LOVE & BOBA

Colin Pennywick

LOVE

&

BOBA

Colin Pennywick

A Mount Oolie Romance

Love & Boba (Love & Boba, Book #1)

Enchanted Woods Publishing

ISBN Print: 9798846010741

First edition, November 2022

Dear Miss Oolie,

What makes my neck so
doughy that it requires kneading?

~ Colin

LOVE & BOBA

CHAPTER 1

Devon slouched against the back of the counter as yet another unsatisfied customer brought his drink back. He sighed loudly as his coworker on shift listened to the complaint and offered to fix it. Was "fixing" it really necessary? Devon had done just what the customer asked, it just didn't happen to be as sweet or milky as the customer wanted.

He bitterly watched as his blonde coworker flashed the customer a smile and took the drink. His coworker, Robbie, was about as sickly sweet as they came. Robbie could smile to your face and act like your best friend, but as soon as Robbie turned and faced Devon, he saw that derisive look. He shot daggers back, not losing in a glaring battle to someone so two-faced. Even when Devon had first started, he'd glared at Robbie from the moment they first met, maybe it was the preppy clothes, or the perfectly gelled hair, but Devon couldn't stand him. Back then, Robbie had given him nothing but smiles and pretended to pout when Devon didn't respond. After a week, Robbie dropped the facade entirely.

"What was wrong this time?" he snapped. He stood right in Robbie's way. The cafe behind the counter wasn't large, but it wasn't small either. There was enough space for two people comfortably, but three people would be climbing over each other to reach the different ingredients and mixer glasses. The cafe itself was brightly lit with a couple unfinished wooden tables and plants everywhere. Most of the cafe space was dedicated to the customers, not the employees.

"Clearly, you just can't get anything right." Robbie stalked right up to Devon and shoved the drink into his hand. "You might as well drink this. I have to make another one. You used the wrong kind of milk."

"Well fuck me for switching the bottles by accident." Devon grabbed an extra wide straw and shoved it in the lid. He took a long slurp, watching Robbie make the drink again from behind the midnight blue hair that was falling in front of his face. His shoulders rounded forward as he leaned against the back counter, blocking the sink.

"Why are you even here?" Robbie glanced at Devon.

"The fuck does that mean?" Devon said with a mouth full of tapioca pearls.

"I'm so telling Kieran about how bad you're doing today." Robbie gave Devon a

2

dirty look. He quickly hid it as he turned back to the customer to hand him the corrected drink.

Devon took another long sip of his drink. He did not need Robbie telling Kieran about this incident. Kieran had known his mom for a long time and when Devon suddenly showed up back home, she'd begged Kieran to give him a job. Devon didn't want to take the job, or any job for that matter, but Kieran had been so nice when he came for an interview, and working in a cafe sounded chill. It normally was, except for the busy times. Which felt like every shift to Devon. If Kieran knew he was fucking up this badly, surely that favor for his mom would run out.

"If you do, I'll tell Kieran about you," Devon finally said after a minute had passed. The customer had gone back to their table by the window and the crawling ivy that lined the walls. The whole cafe was permeated with a fruity smell, such a mix of flavors that a particular scent couldn't be deciphered from another.

Robbie stopped cleaning the counter, putting his hand with the dirty rag on his hip. "Excuse me? Tell Kieran what?"

"That you're an ass."

"The customers love me!" Robbie threw the rag at Devon.

He turned slightly, letting the rag hit his shoulder and fall to the ground. He looked to his shoulder, his hoodie was only a little wet, but Devon made a show of wiping his jacket off anyways. He didn't even bother to pick the rag up, just kept sucking more boba out of the cup. "I don't."

"Who cares what you think." Robbie started pouting, his squishy features scrunching together. Devon had the feeling that it was supposed to earn some sympathy, but it just made him look like a whiny five year old.

Devon didn't talk to Robbie for the rest of his shift. He kept glancing at the clock. The last hour of his shift seemed to drag on forever. On the bright side, whenever a customer did walk in, Robbie went right to the register and didn't even give Devon a chance to make anything. Devon knew that Robbie would end up using this as more ammunition, but he didn't feel like working, so it didn't bother him that much.

When the shift was finally over, Devon was the first one to leave. He left Robbie with the cleanup and locking up the shop. After all, Devon had only been in this job for a few weeks now, he didn't have Kieran's trust with the cafe keys.

"Hey! Stay and finish the work!" Robbie yelled after him, but Devon didn't stop.

He shoved his hands into the pockets of his black, very well-worn hoodie and kept walking home. His slouchy beanie covered up the way his hair showed a different color at the roots from where his hair had grown since he last dyed it. This particular beanie was hand-knit. He'd grown quite a collection of hand-knit beanies. Once his mom realized how much Devon wore them back in high school, she'd always knit him new ones as gifts.

His feet carried himself down the gray, downtown streets. No use taking a bus, he'd been saving all the money he'd been earning, not even getting personal things. He was very glad that his mom wasn't kicking him out any time soon.

He veered off the busy downtown street, heading for the Tree Streets neighborhood. More and more trees started to line the sidewalk and the first of the spring blooms were forming on the branches. He'd lived there with his mom all his life. His dad had stayed until he was twelve and left when Devon's type became more apparent. The first house on the corner belonged to an elderly man who was currently sitting on the porch. The old man waved, so Devon waved back, but he didn't linger. Devon was told that a whole family used to live there, but the wife died before he was born and the kids had all since grown up and moved out. A part of Devon thought it was a waste. It was a nice, big house with a large, now-unkempt, yard. Not like the mansions over in Plum Manor, but bigger than the two bedroom house his mom had.

He sighed to himself, knowing that he shouldn't complain. He could very well still be stuck in the big city, living off of some stranger's wallet. Being home was better than that. He kept walking down the street, his shoes dragging with every step. He finally came across his street, Pine. He took a left and kept walking, he'd known almost all the kids on this block when he was growing up. Played in the streets together. But a lot of them had left for college too. Devon felt conspicuous to be the one who came back to Mount Oolie first.

He skipped up the steps to his mom's two-story house. It looked a lot bigger from the outside with such a wide porch. He'd been hoping to avoid any nosy neighbors, but he wasn't so lucky. Mark, the next door neighbor, walked out right as Devon was walking up.

"Devon! I haven't seen you in a while. Finished college already?"

"Something like that." Devon skirted the topic. He couldn't tell anyone he'd flunked or he'd just bring shame to his mother. He wasn't proud of the things he did to try and pass his classes. In the end, it was such a waste and he never even got a real first relationship before he bartered his way to better grades.

"Will's taking his sweet time at college, won't even come home to visit on holidays," Mark mused. Even though Mark was an alpha, he was one of the most gentle fathers Devon had met. If only his own father had been so understanding…

"Yeah… classes can be busy." He fumbled with his keys, trying to get inside as quickly as he could.

"I wouldn't mind if he at least called once in a while," Mark kept talking. Devon cursed under his breath, could the older man really not take a hint?

Devon finally got the door open. "Sorry, but my mom's waiting."

"Do say Hi to her for me! I missed her at the last club meeting. I really should catch up with her." Devon was already most of the way inside the house by the time Mark finished talking.

He nodded. "Yeah. See ya." He quickly shut the door behind him. He let out a long breath and slumped against the back of the door.

"You don't have to be so rude." His mom's voice made him stand straight up. She was leaning against the archway to the living room, looking right at Devon.

"He wouldn't stop talking." Devon immediately got defensive.

"You weren't out there for more than a minute. He's our neighbor and my friend." She let out a sigh and walked up to Devon. The end of her ponytail brushed against the shoulder of her hand-knit sweater. Devon realized it was the same yarn that she'd used for the beanie he was wearing. He immediately pulled the hat off his head. "How was work today?"

"Fine." Devon tried to walk past her.

She caught his arm, looking up at him. "If you don't like it, why did you leave college? I love having you back home, but I know you."

"Isn't this better? I don't know what I want to do, so why waste money we don't have?" Devon pulled his arm from her grip without looking at her and headed for the stairs.

"Dinner will be ready soon, get washed up."

"Okay, okay…" Devon trudged up the stairs, hands shoved in his pockets again. The walls were lined with family photos, spaces conspicuously empty where his dad had been in the photo and his mom had removed him. Each photo was like a passage through time, showcasing Devon from a toddler all the way up to his mom dropping him off for college. He stopped at the last frame and took it off the wall. His mom had such a proud smile in the photo, nothing like the constant looks of concern he got now. He set the frame face down on the hall table before ducking into his room.

CHAPTER 2

Connor was sitting in his office, fiddling with the pen in his hand. Everyone had already gone to lunch, but he was staring out of the glass windows of his office at the rest of the empty company. Despite his startup being fairly new, it was already successful enough to take up the largest space in the office building. The whole floor was rented out to OroBRS, his financial technology startup pioneering a new kind of lending system. The space was designed to be open, no cubicles, no assigned desks, even though teams self-assigned anyways. The open workspaces felt so desolate when no one was at the desks. Only laptops and monitors cluttered the space, constantly emitting a low, whirring hum. He let out a long breath. This was his one moment he had alone and didn't have to show up strong for everyone else.

His own lunch was packed neatly in a box and sitting untouched on his desk. His administrative assistant, Sammy, always assumed his girlfriend made it for him. But he was the one who always made it for himself and took the time and care to have a decent presentation. He always put his best foot forward, even for himself. His office was rather sparse, with only a desk, a few chairs, and a spider plant he kept in the corner. It was supposed to help brighten his day since he'd kept anything personal out of his office. The glass windows and door certainly made the space feel bigger, but it cost almost everything in terms of privacy. He'd waited too long to even eat his lunch because a few people were already filing back into the office. Teams were sitting down to work, happily chatting as they got started. He was lucky that his business was thriving. Only 100 employees and his startup was already worth $1 million. He worked with friends, had competent employees. He should be happy.

But he wasn't.

Sammy was just sitting down at his desk, so Connor quickly sat up and covered his lunch. Better to keep his internal emotions to himself. Sammy, with as cheery a smile as always, knocked on his office door right as Connor was storing his lunchbox back into his messenger bag. Connor motioned for him to enter.

"Riley is asking to meet with you today. It seems urgent, would you like me to shuffle your meetings this afternoon?" His smile became a little more nervous and he ruffled his fingers through his short black hair.

Connor nodded. "Yes, I'll go talk to her now, clear my schedule for the day."

"For the rest of the day?" Sammy raised his brow, blinking a few times.

"Yes." He stood up, pushing his shoulders back and taking a few decisive steps out from behind his desk. Sammy nodded, hunched his shoulders, and scurried back to his own desk. Connor let out a small laugh, did he seem that intimidating? It wasn't a bad thing, but Sammy had been his assistant for over a year now, he would've thought Sammy would be used to him.

Connor walked to a cluster of desks by the windows where Riley, and the rest of the finance team, had their desks. The rest of the team were already busy at work around her. "Should we talk in my office?"

Riley jolted for a moment, she'd been head down at her computer until Connor walked up. She looked up at him, the fringe of her pixie cut falling in front of her forehead. She smiled. "Yeah, it shouldn't take too long."

Connor shook his head. "Finance conversations are never short." She was the CFO after all. He and Riley had even gone to college together. He was the one who convinced her to move to Mount Oolie to join his startup.

Riley walked into his office first and waited for Connor to shut the door. She let out a long breath and sat in the comfy chair next to his desk. "I actually don't want to talk about finances. We're doing just fine, you'll have all the numbers you need for the next investor meeting."

Connor furrowed his brow and sat down in the wooden chair next to his desk that was for guests. He fixed a few strands of his deep, rose red hair that had fallen out of place. At first glance, he looked like a 1950's businessman, but the close-shaved sides gave him a modern edge. He angled the chair towards her and leaned back, his back to the door, so no one outside his office could see his expression. Rolling up the sleeves of his off white button up shirt, he asked, "Then what is it?"

"I… happened to see you in here before I went to lunch," she paused for a moment, as if slowly thinking over what to say.

"I always eat lunch in here." He crossed his arms over his chest. Nothing was wrong with bringing lunch from home. Maybe it wasn't typical of alphas to do so, but he wasn't traditional. He didn't need to be bothered by the noisy people that frequented the cafeteria-style lunch spot that was so popular with everyone in the whole building.

She looked at him with both brow raised and a sad smile on her lips. "You didn't used to. You would go to lunch with me and Jeremy. Sometimes even Kameron would come along."

"I get more work done when I eat in here." Connor shrugged, avoiding eye contact. He'd been trying to make it look like he was too busy to go out for lunch. If Riley could see through him so easily, how many other employees also noticed? He leaned back in the chair rubbing his chin, this wouldn't do at all. Was he going to have to go out for lunch now simply because it's what people expected?

"Is that what you call what you were doing when you were twirling your pen between your fingers a few moments ago?" She sat up straighter.

"What, I can't think for a moment?" He uncrossed his arms and threw his hands up, still refusing to look directly at her.

"I'm just saying that I know it's been hard since Zach left."

"He didn't leave. It was a mutual decision that it wasn't working anymore." She'd barely finished speaking before Connor replied. He should've guessed that this was where the conversation was going. He didn't mean to snap at Riley, but he couldn't dwell on losing Zach while he was at work. The breakup had been a quiet one, their entire relationship had been understated and never very public. It didn't seem like it would make too much of an impact when they stopped seeing one another. Zach had told him that he didn't want to be together anymore and he'd only stayed with Connor for the money, but he'd found someone else where it was about love too. The whole thing had been quite shocking to Connor. He had always taken Zach out to nice places on their dates, always brought flowers. Sometimes he'd have to reschedule because of a crisis at work, but Zach knew that Connor had a startup. But by the time Zach left, he would hardly send a message to Connor, only reaching out if he needed something.

Riley leaned back in her seat, using her firm, presenter voice with him, "All I'm saying is that I've seen you wallowing in here during lunch every day and I think it's time you stop."

"What if you are right? How am I supposed to just stop?" Connor insisted. He didn't much care for being told to move on, even if it had already been months.

"I have a few ideas." She smirked and stood up. "Let's walk and talk about it."

He quirked a brow and looked up at her. "Coffee break so soon after lunch?"

"Do you really want to talk about this with Sammy sitting right outside?"

He glanced over his shoulder at Sammy. His assistant seemed preoccupied with his own work and it was unlikely that he'd overhear anything. But Connor knew that look in Riley's eyes. It most likely meant that their conversation would take a turn that would be best kept out of a workplace setting.

"Alright," he grumbled and stood up, too. "Where should we go?"

"I know this great cafe." She went to the door and walked out without waiting for Connor. He quickly grabbed his phone and keys and followed her out and closed the door behind him.

They walked out of the office, their departure not turning a head. They were the company executives after all. Connor followed Riley down to the street level of Mount Oolie's small downtown. It may have been an odd place to have a startup, but the rent was much cheaper than being in a big city, and so was the cost of living. But the real reason was that Connor had an attachment to being home. As long as he'd lived here, there were still spots he didn't know. It was rather embarrassing that Riley knew more of the hidden gems than he did.

"Maybe we could take you out to a bar? Meet someone new?" She looked up at him as they walked.

"That sounds so cold to meet someone in a bar." Really, Connor was just making excuses.

"You have to be open to meeting someone new." She nudged his side.

He looked down at her, expression as serious as he could be. "What if I don't want to meet someone new?"

She tilted her head to the side. "Is that true, or do you just not want to let go of Zach?"

"Fuck." She clearly knew him too well. He looked straight ahead again. "Just don't go setting me up. If I meet someone, I'll meet someone."

He hadn't even been paying attention to the shops they walked by and was about to keep walking straight down the sidewalk, but Riley stopped him and ushered him inside a cafe. It was brightly lit and filled with plants, giving off a very down-to-earn vibe. Once inside, he saw two guys behind the counter. He could tell they were both omegas, the scent was oddly strong to him, even if he was an alpha. There was a large chalkboard menu on the wall behind the counter with a printed logo with the words "Almond Blossom Tea" overlaying some flowers.

He looked down at Riley, furrowing his brow. "This is the spot?"

She chuckled and nodded. "They have good boba."

"I haven't tried boba."

"Then now's as good a time as any to try it." She smiled and strolled right up to the counter. The blonde employee was the one at the register. It seemed like the bluenette was determined to stand in the background and glower. "Two okinawa milk teas with boba."

"But I don't know what I want." He whispered to Riley.

She smiled. "It's a classic flavor, try a regular one before getting too creative."

He chuckled and pulled out his wallet, handing his card over to the cashier. The cashier thanked them. Connor and Riley turned to walk to a table, but Connor heard a bunch of plastic toppling over and looked back. The two employees seemed to be fighting over the drink cups. Finally, the bluenette stole the two cups and snapped, "I got it, okay?!"

He chuckled to himself and joined Riley at a window table.

"Maybe we should go out this weekend? I can invite Sam too." Riley smiled.

"Great, making me a third wheel with you and your boyfriend is a great way for me to meet someone." He let out a long sigh.

"We could do something else." She kept talking and making suggestions, but Connor was only half listening. He kept looking back to the counter and watching the bluenette make the drinks. The barista kept fumbling and almost dropping the cups or the milk cartons. It took him back to high school when he'd first started cooking for himself and would make such a mess in the kitchen. He smiled to himself. "What are you looking at?" Riley's words jarred Connor back to the present.

"Hmm?" He looked back at her.

"Did you even hear anything I said?"

"Actually…" He thought about lying, but chose not to. "No. I just… there's something about the barista making our drinks."

"You mean how he hardly seems to know what he's doing?"

"No, I don't know, maybe. He seems… wholesome." Connor looked back at the barista whose eyes brightened and had such a satisfied smile when he was finally putting the lids on the drinks. Even from across the room, it made Connor smile too. Connor stood up from the table. "I'll be right back."

CHAPTER 3

Devon wrestled the cups away from Robbie. He didn't know why he even cared so much. He'd been slacking the entire shift until the tall redhead walked in. There was something about him that made Devon's heart flutter. Maybe it was the broad shoulders or the chiseled cheeks or the swept back red hair... Robbie had given him the strangest look when Devon had even reached for the cups at all.

The drinks weren't anything fancy, but that didn't seem to help Devon. He fumbled through the whole process, almost spilling the drinks a few times, but he managed to finish making the drinks and seal the plastic lids onto the cups. He was just putting the cups onto the pick-up counter, about to call out the order name, when Devon looked up and was face to face with the handsome redhead.

"Are these for me?" The redhead's lips twitched up into a smile.

Devon gulped. Damn, how did the redhead do that? Catch him off guard just enough... He stood up straight. Even though he was tall, the redhead was taller. "Well, they're for that chick you're sitting with. How should I know if they're for you?"

"Don't worry, one of them certainly is." He took a straw and unwrapped it before slipping it through the lid. The redhead took a drink, his lips pursing and his eyes squinting. But the expression was soon gone. "Are you sure it's supposed to taste like this?"

"I did it the exact way it's supposed to be!" He snapped a little too loudly, getting Robbie to look over at him and the redhead. He crossed his arms, not wanting to be called out for making a bad drink.

"Did you taste it?"

"We can't try our customer's drinks."

"You can try mine." Devon blinked up at the redhead a few times, looking right into those ruby eyes. The man smiled. "I won't tell if you won't." He held the drink out to Devon.

At this close of a range, he could feel the scent coming off of the man and knew he was an alpha. He was annoyed at himself for being so subject to his baser instincts as to be interested in the man just because he was an alpha, but even more annoyed in himself for swiping the drink from the man's hand. He sipped from the same straw that had been in the redhead's lips not moments ago. Could he actually taste the redhead or was he imagining that? Either way, the drink itself did taste pretty bland. But Devon handed the drink back. "It's fine as it is."

"Is that so?" The alpha raised a brow.

"I'm not remaking it," Devon straight up refused.

An audible sigh came from behind Devon and Robbie strolled up next to him and smiled at the alpha. Since they were both omegas, something about Devon's space being invaded by Robbie made him aggressively upset. Robbie smiled and leaned forward a bit, offering his hand out to the alpha. "I can make your drink properly, sir."

But the man shook his head. "No thank you." He looked at Devon. "I'm sorry, I didn't get your name."

"Devon."

The alpha smiled. "No replacement will be necessary, Devon made the drink the way it's supposed to be."

Both omegas blinked at the man. But he smiled back and looked right at Devon. "I do need one other thing though."

"Yeah?"

"What's your number?"

Devon gulped, he hadn't expected this, even if he did accidentally try to get the redhead's attention. "I don't even know your name."

"Connor." He got out a business card and wrote a number on the back of it. "Call me. I'll make a drink for you next time."

Devon took the card, still staring up at Connor. Connor smiled and walked back to his table with the lady. It wasn't until Robbie jabbed him the ribs that he finally looked away. "What was that for?!"

"You asshole!"

"Me?" Devon smacked Robbie back.

"You're just stealing the attention of all the hot customers!"

"He came on to me!"

"But I was supposed to make those drinks." Robbie pouted.

Devon's nose curled. "So? If he wanted to go to you, he would have. It's not like I'm going to call him. Take the stupid card."

"Did you even look at it?" Robbie put his hands on his hips.

Devon hadn't actually looked. He took a moment to look down. He was holding the card face up, the golden logo of OroBRS was embossed on the card and covering half of it. Under the logo was the name Connor Thorton, written under the name, it said "CEO and Founder". Devon blinked again. Did he really get the number of the CEO of the biggest startup in Mount Oolie?

Robbie snatched the card from Devon's hands, smirking.

"H-hey!" Devon reached for the card, but Robbie stepped back.

"No take backs! You said you weren't going to call him." Robbie looked at the back of the card. "I think I will."

Devon was about to run at him for it, but Robbie slipped it into his pocket and rushed back to the register to help the next wave of customers coming in. Devon glanced over to Connor's table where he seemed deep in conversation with his friend, or was she his friend? Either way, he didn't seem to notice Robbie stealing the card. Devon was relieved, he didn't want to blow it already.

Throughout the rest of the shift, he kept trying to sneak up to Robbie, reaching for the pocket, but every time he got close, Robbie elbowed him aside. Devon didn't work at all for the rest of his shift, just followed Robbie around, trying to get the card back. Quickly, their shift was over and for the first time, Robbie was the one to leave first, leaving the rest of the cleaning for Devon.

Devon kept muttering to himself all the while cleaning. He had never been able to get that card back and probably lost the only chance he'll have at talking to the CEO again. If it wasn't meant to happen, he couldn't help it, but damn, it would've been nice if something could go his way.

He must've been taking too long cleaning because he heard a knock on the front door and looked up. He'd already locked it and put the closed sign up, so who was knocking? He walked closer and saw his mom through the glass. He let out a breath and opened the door up for her.

"Mom, what's the matter?"

"I've been waiting for over an hour, you never came home." Her brow was creased with worry and she touched his cheek. "Is everything okay?"

He nodded slowly and looked back at her. "Yeah, it's just that my shift partner already left for the day."

"You know, the cafe is doing so well, I don't see why Kieran can't hire more employees." She let out a long sigh. "Are you almost done?"

"I'm 20, Mom…" He held the broom he was holding a little tighter and looked to the side.

"And you're living at home. So the least you can do is tell me that you'll be late for dinner." She looked back up at him. "Are you done?"

He bit his lip and nodded. "Yeah, let's go home." He put the broom behind the counter then joined his mom by the door again.

They walked out of the shop and Devon locked the door behind him. Robbie was thoughtful enough to leave behind the shop keys. Unfortunately, this meant that Devon would have to go in early tomorrow. He walked quietly home with his mom, not saying a word.

● ● ●

It was far too early in the morning for anyone to be out, at least in Devon's opinion. Sure, it was barely eight in the morning, but Devon was not a morning person and if he could sleep until noon he would. But today was not one of those days. He was already on his way back to the café to return the store keys.

He hoped that someone was there because he didn't want to open the shop and have to start working. Luckily, by the time he was approaching the café, the doors were already open. The owner, Kieran, was already inside. If Devon had known that the owner would actually show up this morning, he probably would have slept until noon after all. He let out a long breath and went inside the café.

"Kieran?"

The owner looked up from where he was stocking cups behind the counter, his auburn hair swished in front of his face as he moved. He smiled at Devon, laughing slightly as he said, "I didn't expect to see you here at all."

"Do you only work mornings or what? I guess I wouldn't be here if Robbie hadn't left the stupid keys." Devon strolled in and leaned against the front counter. "Ugh, it's so hard to work with him."

"Funny. He says the same thing about you," Kieran said with a smirk.

Devon stood straight up. "He said he wouldn't complain about me to you! I know I'm not the best employee, but I really need this job. Don't fire me because of him."

Kieran laughed and shook his head. "I'm not going to fire you." Kieran stopped laughing and rested a hand on his hip, his hazel eyes piercing right through Devon. "Though I am curious why you're the one with the keys to my shop when it should be Robbie."

"Well…" Devon looked to the side. "So, a customer gave me something, Robbie took it and left so I couldn't get it back from him…" That was more or less what happened, right? He wasn't sure if it was quite appropriate to tell the shop owner that a customer gave him his number.

Kieran furrowed his brow, clearly unhappy about Devon's statement. "What did the customer give you and if Robbie's taking things, maybe I should talk to him."

"I'm not trying to get Robbie fired either!" Devon covered his face with his hands. He fished the keys out of his pocket and tossed them onto the counter. "Can I go home now?"

"What are you not telling me?" Kieran took the keys and put them in his pocket. He leaned over the counter, staring right into Devon's dark blue eyes.

"It doesn't matter." Devon took a step back and turned to the door. "I'll be back for my shift."

"You're lucky I'm so easy on you, most bosses wouldn't be," Kieran called after him, but Devon didn't turn around.

CHAPTER 4

Connor was in the kitchen of Rose Gold, the newest restaurant in downtown Mount Oolie. It was an upscale place with nothing but the freshest fare and the best ingredients. The kitchen was no less spectacular with shiny, new equipment and a space for everything. He'd gone to high school with the chef, Tristan, and even helped his friend invest in the restaurant to get it off the ground. It was in the middle of the dinner rush, but Connor had been in the kitchen since he left the office early to come see his friend. He leaned against the counter next to where Tristan was preparing some dishes.

Connor had been holding his phone in his hands, staring at it as if that could make it ring. He suddenly looked at Tristan. "Was it stupid to give him my number like that?"

Tristan looked up, shrugging. "No. You took a shot, that's what matters." Tristan was just as tall as Connor and also had red hair, though his was more fiery and always pulled back into a samurai bun. Back in high school, kids called them Ruby and Rosie. It was supposed to be an insult since they never did anything their traditionalist school expected of alphas.

Tristan would bite off anyone's head who called them that to their face, but Connor never gave it much weight.

"I feel stupid for waiting for him to call." But after seeing Devon earlier that day, he could think of nothing else. He couldn't even get work done. His mind had been too busy imagining different date scenarios with Devon.

"So don't wait." Tristan wiped his hands off and snatched the phone from Connor.

"And now how will I know if he calls?" He clicked his tongue, annoyed with his friend.

"See? This is why I needed to do this." Tristan laughed. He stopped prepping the food and leaned against the counter. "You're acting so soft."

"Fuck you, I'm not soft." Connor stood up straighter and crossed his arms over his chest.

"Maybe some omegas are into a squishy alpha." Tristan smirked, also crossing his arms over his chest too.

"Really fuck you. Why are you so bitter?"

"We have a lot of bad reviews…"

"What?" Connor furrowed his brow because of the sudden topic change.

"The restaurant, there's a lot of negative ones lately." Tristan dragged his hand down his face. "People keep coming here, but I can't even look at Yelp anymore."

"It can't be that bad if people are still coming?" This was news to Connor. He should be more involved as an investor, but it was mostly so he could enjoy his friend's cooking.

"There's a bunch from the same guy."

"The same guy?"

Tristan nodded. "BluePlate5pecial. He leaves a ton of reviews and he's already left 5 on my place. But he's so weird because apparently each review is from a separate visit."

"Why does he bother coming back?"

"Hell if I know. I don't even know what he looks like. I wish I could find him in the restaurant one of these days and give him a piece of my mind," Tristan snapped.

"We'll be fine. People still love the food here." Connor patted his friend's shoulder.

Tristan shoved the phone back in Connor's hand. "Your stupid phone call is coming in."

Connor took the phone and looked down at the screen as it rang. He didn't recognize the number, but it was a local area code. He answered the call. "Hello?"

"Hi~! Is this Connor?" An overly sweet voice rang in Connor's ears. He'd only spoken to Devon that little bit, but he knew that this was not the same voice. "We met at the Almond Blossom Tea shop today."

"Who's calling." Connor was very unamused. Had Devon given away his number to this guy?

"It's Robbie from the cafe. Devon's coworker." He could hear the smile in Robbie's voice, but it unsettled Connor.

"Yes. And why are you calling?" Tristan was staring at Connor, brow furrowed.

"I was hoping I could take you up on that offer." Robbie paused before speaking again. "I'm much better with drinks than Devon."

"I see, well thank you for calling, but I'm afraid I'll have to say no." Connor responded in his monotone business voice he used when he was rejecting a business deal. "Goodbye." He hung up the phone and tossed it on the counter.

"I assume that wasn't the barista?"

"He gave my number away." Connor was fuming, hands gripping onto the edge of the counter to keep himself from lashing out.

Tristan rested his hand on Connor's shoulder. "Connor, I'm—"

Connor cut him off and shrugged his hand off his shoulder. "I'm going home." He turned and started to walk out of the kitchen without even waiting for a response. He shoved his hands in his pockets as he skulked out of the restaurant all together. He'd definitely gotten his hopes up too soon, but Devon's face had been too cute to resist. He barely remembered what the other guy looked like.

He was taking his time to walk home, going the long way which led him across the street from Almond Blossom Tea. He stopped, watching Devon sweeping up and soon leaving the cafe with an older woman. He quickly resumed walking before Devon could see him. He didn't need the young omega thinking he was a stalker, too.

• • •

Connor was sitting in his office again, spinning a pen over his fingers. He kept tapping the desk with his other hand, a sour expression on his face. He'd had the same look all morning, which put every attendee of his meetings more on edge. Everyone seemed to think he was displeased with the company's progress, but Connor was still angry about Devon.

Now that most people were heading out for lunch, Connor stood up. He tossed the pen on his desk, the immaculate organization of his desk ruined. He went to the office door and yanked it open. His assistant jolted in his seat and looked back at Connor. "Is something wrong, sir?"

33

"No." Connor kept walking to Riley's desk. "We're going to Almond Blossom."

She slowly turned from her computer, blinking a few times as she looked up at him. She finally furrowed her brow and asked, "What?"

"Lunch. Let's go." He turned and walked away without seeing if she was actually following him.

She saved her work on her computer and stood up. Grabbing her bag, she jogged a few steps to catch up to Connor. "What's going on?"

Connor waited until they were out of the main office and in the elevator going down. "I have someone I need to talk to and if I get out of hand, I need you there."

"Someone you need to talk to? Is it that barista from yesterday?"

"Yeah, I have something to straighten out."

She let out a sigh and rubbed the back of her neck. "If he said no, why are we going back?"

"He said yes, but he let someone else take his chance."

"You lost me." She rubbed her forehead.

"It doesn't matter. If he's there, I need to talk to him."

"And if he's not?" Riley raised one brow.

"I'll find out when he is." Connor didn't say anything else, he started walking as soon as the elevator doors opened. He didn't make small talk or acknowledge anyone else on the street. He beelined for the cafe and went right through the doors.

The blonde barista was at the register, smiling until Connor stalked up to the counter. "Where's Devon?"

"I-in the back." Robbie gulped, staring up at Connor. "I-I can get him?"

"Could you please?" Riley added with a smile and a soft tone.

Riley sighed. There was no turning off Connor's intimidating aura today. Connor's behavior was clearly enough to scare any omega. Devon seeing him in such a state could completely scare him off. She pulled Connor aside as Robbie ducked into the back of the cafe. "Can you please calm down? You're scaring everyone here."

Connor glanced around and noticed that he was getting quite a few glances from other people in the cafe. He shrugged. "You're not scared."

She rolled her eyes. "Because I know you."

Connor had to admit that she had a point. But he still wanted to see Devon and tell him off for giving his card away. He took a deep breath, waiting for Devon to come out.

Finally, Devon stepped out from the back and stared right at Connor, eyes wide. Connor could see his Adam's apple move as he gulped. Devon spun on his heel, about to go to the back again, but almost ran into Robbie.

"Don't go anywhere just yet." Connor's tone was commanding. He didn't mean to be, but sometimes as an alpha, it just seeped out. Devon reluctantly turned back around and went to join Connor at the counter. "You don't want to see me so much that you want to hide from me?"

"What are you even talking about? You're the one acting weird at a cafe," Devon mumbled and pulled his beanie further down his forehead, pushing his hair to shield his eyes. He slouched against the counter.

"I would rather have gotten no call at all than a call from someone else."

"I can't control who's calling you." Devon deliberately avoided eye contact.

"You can when you're the one who gave them my number." Connor leaned over the counter, getting closer to Devon.

"I didn't give it away…" Devon mumbled again, fidgeting with his arms. "He took it and ran." Devon stood up straight and glared right at Connor. "You know, it's pretty ballsy of you to just walk in here and come at me like this."

Connor's brow raised. He'd never met an omega who talked back to him like that. He smiled, his own tension relaxing. "I'm only human."

"A dumb one." Devon's lower lip jutted out.

"Excuse me?"

"Why'd you have to do this here? I don't want to lose my job for arguing with a customer."

That pouty look on Devon's face was too cute for Connor. He chuckled and extended his hand to Devon. "I don't want you to lose your job." Devon reached towards Connor, but pulled his hand away at the last minute. "Would you have called me?"

"If you keep asking, I might say no."

Connor chuckled and nodded. "Then let me ask this instead. Want to go to dinner with me tonight?"

"I dunno, can you wait until I'm off work to bother me again?" Devon chuckled a bit.

"On my word." Connor held up a hand.

"Then come back when the cafe closes." Devon smiled. "That's when I'll be done."

CHAPTER 5

Devon hung up his apron on the rack in the back, humming to himself. He didn't think he'd be so excited to go out with Connor. He hardly knew more than his name, but the idea of being pursued actually made him happy. Still, trusting an alpha to behave was a risk. He'd made that mistake before and he was not about to do that again. No matter how charming the alpha was, he wasn't going to go home with him. Not on the first date.

"Pretty happy with yourself, aren't you?" Robbie's voice drifted from behind him.

"What is it now, Robbie?" Devon rolled his eyes, not bothering to turn around.

But Robbie walked up and leaned against the wall next to him, right in Devon's sights. "You think you're all hot shit because that guy came back for you today, don't you?"

Devon shook his head and strolled to the door.

"You're not Cinderella and he's not your Prince Charming," Robbie called after him.

Devon stopped in his tracks. "Do you ever have a positive thing to say to me?"

"I would if you deserved it."

"You're as bitter as our coffee." Devon swung the door open and went back to behind the counter. Even though they were closing up, there were still a couple customers they were waiting on to leave. Devon thought about just going home, Robbie's words ringing in his ears. No, he wasn't going to purposely miss his date with Connor... Connor what? He'd forgotten his last name and Robbie never gave him the business card back. A pit grew in Devon's stomach. Was going out with a stranger really a good idea? Going out with someone he knew had even turned out risky.

Devon didn't have time to think about those bad dates. Movement in the corner of his eyes caught Devon's attention. Connor was already strolling up, he walked with such purpose and his shoulders pushed back. Even through the store window, Devon could see that big grin on the redhead's face. The ball of nerves building up in his stomach was threatening to make him lose his lunch. He quickly turned around and tried to duck into the back room, even if Robbie was in there. But the bells chimed as the store door opened.

Connor's deep voice drifted from behind him, "Hello, Devon."

"Hey..." Devon bit his lip and took a breath before turning around. He would not be swayed by an alpha's voice. No matter how deep and sexy it sounded and how amazing it would feel to have it whispered in his ear... shit, Devon really needed to get a hold of himself. "You're early."

"I believe it's eight p.m. on the dot." Connor walked up to the counter, resting his arms over the edge of it and leaning towards Devon.

"Isn't being punctual considered early?" Devon held Connor's gaze, refusing to back down, despite those growing nerves telling him to run.

Connor raised a brow. "Would it be better to be late and make you wonder if i'm going to show up at all?"

Connor was right about that. Devon would definitely not prefer it. But Devon couldn't admit that. He shrugged and gestured to the last two customers still chatting at a table. "Can't leave yet."

"What about the blonde guy from earlier? Did he leave already?"

Devon chuckled. "Robbie. And no, he's in the back."

Connor smirked. "Then leave it to him and come with me."

"You can be really demanding even though I hardly know you." Devon didn't mean it in a good or bad way. Perhaps it was more that it was expected of an alpha, but Devon always hoped there would be some who weren't so… controlling.

Connor let out a long breath. "I know what I want. Is that bad?"

"Am I just something you want?" Devon crossed his arms, looking right at Connor.

"You were happy to go on a date with me earlier, what changed?" Connor stood up straight, furrowing his brow.

"I just…" Devon finally looked away. "I don't know you."

"Isn't that why you should go on a date with me? Get to know me?" Connor chuckled. "It's just dinner at a restaurant not far from here, I'm not inviting you on a cruise or anywhere private."

Devon's shoulders relaxed and he looked back at Connor. He did make a good point, Devon couldn't deny that. "Just dinner then."

"Just dinner." Connor smiled and pushed his broad shoulders back. He waited for Devon to walk out from behind the counter and extended his hand to him.

Devon blinked at his hand a few times. "I'm not a dainty damsel."

"I know." Connor kept offering his hand. Devon sighed and took it as they left the cafe together.

Connor led them down a few streets, further into downtown and into a swanky restaurant. Devon had heard about Rose Gold opening, but it was an upscale place and one that he couldn't afford on his barista's paycheck. He stopped and looked up when they reached the door. Connor noticed and looked back at Devon. He smiled and gently tugged on Devon's hand. Devon gulped and took a few steps forward. Connor better be paying or he'd be in big trouble.

The inside was elegantly decorated with modern art on the walls and mood lighting and candles on every table. Definitely a good spot for a date, Devon had to admit that Connor had taste.

Connor strolled right up to the host stand and asked for a table for two. Without hesitation, the host promised them the best table. Did Connor come here a lot? No way Devon belonged in a fancy place like this. How far through the date would they get before Connor realized it? Devon scooted closer to Connor, sticking as close as he could and holding his hand rather tightly. That nervous feeling in his stomach refused to settle. He took a deep breath, trying to calm himself and he suddenly smelled bubble tea. How calming, but how odd. He looked up to Connor, seeing the redhead smiling as they were shown to their table—a cozy window table lit only by a candle in the middle and the best view of the street. Devon tried to subtly turn his face towards Connor's arm and take a discreet sniff. The scent of bubble tea seemed to hang on his clothes and mix with the woody scent of his cologne.

Before the host could pull out the chairs, Connor pulled one out for Devon. He stared at it a moment before slowly sitting down. He was still processing being pampered like this, unsure yet as to whether or not he liked it. He was an omega, but he wasn't helpless... even though he had been in bad situations before.

"You must come here a lot," Devon said as Connor sat down across from him.

Connor smiled and looked at Devon for a minute before even responding. "I'm one of the investors."

CHAPTER 6

The expression of shock combined with shyness on Devon's face was enough to melt Connor's heart. But he did his best not to show it. He wasn't normally the kind of person to flaunt his assets, but he really wanted to impress Devon. It had surprised him when Devon had been so resistant to go on the date at all. That was a problem he'd never had with Zach. Maybe a bit of a challenge would be better for him.

Devon swallowed, resuming a neutral expression. "Good for you. I've never really been into the Mount Oolie restaurant scene."

"If you want me to show you which restaurants are good, I'd be happy to." Connor chuckled.

"Let's see how tonight goes first." Devon glanced away and scratched his neck.

"Still unsure about me?" Connor leaned forward. His gaze right on Devon's eyes—such a lovely blue with flecks of what looked silver in the light.

"Aren't you still unsure about me? You don't know me either." Devon chanced a glance back at Connor, but quickly looked down at the table.

"But I'd like to." Connor smiled. "Are you a barista all of the time?"

"No, I'm a stu–" Devon shook his head. "No, I'm between things."

Connor raised a brow, wondering why Devon suddenly changed his words. "Between what things?"

"Finished high school. Not sure about college. Maybe I am just a barista." Devon leaned back and crossed his arms, his lower lip jutting out. "Happy? You're on a date with a lame guy."

Connor didn't want to smile because Devon seemed genuinely upset, but also how could he not smile at such a pouty expression? He took a breath, suppressing the urge. "Really? Because I'm sure there's more to the story than that."

"Nope." Devon kept leaning back until their server came by with some water glasses and a couple of cocktails. Devon's eyes widened at the fancy martini glass with a red liquid in front of him.

The waiter smiled. "Compliments of the chef. Are you both ready to order?"

"Bring us an appetizer, the chef knows which ones." Connor looked up at the waiter and picked up his own drink, a simple manhattan on the rocks, nothing fancy. The waiter smiled and left.

Connor looked back at Devon to find him glaring at him. Devon snapped, "Don't I even get a say? What if I don't want this drink? Which appetizer are you even getting?"

"Would you rather have mine?" He held out his own glass to Devon.

Devon leaned forward and hissed, "I'm 20, I hope that doesn't spoil your plans of getting me drunk tonight."

Even though that had never been his plan, he was surprised that Devon was still under drinking age. Connor set his own drink down and pulled Devon's towards himself too. "Then I'll have yours. You're free to get any drink you'd like."

"All I can afford here is this water." Devon snatched the water glass, spilling some of it on the table.

"You needn't be so crass." Connor's expression darkened. This unhappy side of Devon was not the person he thought he'd be going on a date with. "I asked you out, I will pay for our dinner."

"Yeah, well, you don't have to act like I'm a princess who needs rescuing." Devon took a gulp of water and started choking.

He leaned back, drumming his fingers against the table. "Are you sure you don't need rescuing?"

Devon was finally able to stop coughing. "Shut up."

"If you don't want to be here, you don't have to be." Connor said, completely serious.

Devon shook his head. "I want to be here dammit." Connor raised a brow and crossed his arms, finding that hard to believe. Devon let out a sigh and leaned against the table. "Fucking Robbie."

"What?" Connor furrowed his brow, even more confused than before.

"Right before you got to the cafe, he said I was acting like a fucking princess and here you are treating me like one. I feel pathetic." Devon covered his face with both of his hands.

Connor let out a breath of relief. He reached out to touch Devon's arm. "Would it make you feel better if we went somewhere else and I let you pay your own way?"

Devon shook his head.

Connor smiled, this was the shyness that he found so cute. "Then let's start over from now and forget about Robbie for the night. Okay?"

Devon nodded and slowly took a hand away. Connor caught a glimpse of pink on the omega's cheek before Devon hid his face again.

Slowly, Devon started to relax, but Connor never took his eyes off him. Devon hid behind his hands for a while until the first appetizer, some braised vegetables in a sweet teriyaki glaze, was set on their table. He immediately perked up and dropped his hands. He still avoided looking directly at Connor, but Connor didn't mind. He watched as Devon took the first bite. "So? How is it?"

Devon's gaze finally landed on Connor again. He shrugged a bit and looked away. "It's actually pretty good."

"You just don't want to be wrong, do you?" Connor chuckled and picked up a piece too.

"Do you?" Devon raised his brow and let out a small laugh. It was the first time Connor had seen him so relaxed. Devon really did have such soft yet defined features. By all accounts, he was objectively beautiful. A part of Connor immediately felt the need to keep Devon safe from other men. But he fought the urge rising in his gut, knowing that it was just the alpha in him.

Connor shook his head. "Of course not. But it's not a common trait in omegas."

"Do I seem common to you?" Devon glared back at Connor.

"Not at all." Connor chuckled and leaned forward. "In fact, I think there's quite a lot to you."

"You should! You're the one who asked me out." Devon smiled again and took an unnecessarily large bite.

Connor smiled and sat back to eat, too. When the waiter came back to take their orders, he let Devon make his own order. Devon didn't hesitate in ordering a large dish with a lot of decadent sauces. Connor was glad that Devon wasn't afraid to eat in front of him. Zach had never eaten more than a small salad, it always made Connor wonder if he went home hungry.

"You sound hungry after all." Connor smiled at Devon.

"Yeah, so? You said you'd take me to dinner, so I wanna eat." Devon raised a brow. "Is that another thing I'm not supposed to do as an omega?"

Connor could hear the bite behind Devon's words. He shook his head. "I'm not comparing you to what you should or shouldn't be. I'm learning who you are." Devon's responses did trouble Connor though. Was Devon not happy with his type? He leaned across the table, voice hushed as he asked, "Do you think you should've been an alpha?"

"The hell's with that personal question all of a sudden?" Devon leaned back and crossed his arms over his chest. "No! And I was until I wasn't."

That didn't make any sense to Connor. He only blinked back at Devon, but no further explanation was offered. Connor leaned back and shrugged. "You seem sensitive about it."

"I just don't want to be judged." Devon let out a sigh and reached across the table to take back the red cocktail. He lifted it and took a sip before Connor could stop him.

"I feel like I should take that drink away from you." Connor furrowed his brow.

"I'm close enough to 21, what difference does a couple months make?" Devon took another sip. Given his apparent ease with alcohol, Connor figured this was not the first time Devon drank.

"So your birthday's coming up?"

"Planning that far ahead are you?" Devon smirked.

"What if I was?" He chuckled.

"If it was any other guy, I'd say you're too clingy." Devon leaned across the table, gently touching Connor's hand. "But for some reason it's cute on you and I don't even know why."

Connor smiled and turned his hand to hold Devon's hand. "I'm glad to hear that. I may end up spoiling you."

Connor leaned in too, closing the distance to hover an inch from Devon's lips. "There's something irresistible about you."

"Then maybe don't resist?" Devon responded with a blush.

Connor smiled and leaned in all the way. He kissed Devon deeply, feeling those warm, soft lips against his own.

CHAPTER 7

Devon sleepily rubbed his eyes, blinking as he woke up in unfamiliar surroundings. He looked around the room. He was alone, but he didn't remember where he came back to. He'd been at Rose Gold with Connor, but he'd ended up drinking with him and that first kiss turned into a few more.

A knock came at the door and Devon looked up. He was still dressed, but he pulled the blue satin covers up to cover his body regardless. "Yeah?"

Connor opened the door, even in the morning, he looked so well put together. Did he always have to look that handsome with his hair slicked back? Connor smiled and Devon's heart fluttered. "Sleep well?"

Devon nodded slowly. "Yeah, but umm..." he looked down at himself, biting his lower lip. "Did we?"

Connor shook his head. "If we had, you wouldn't be waking up alone."

"But last night's kind of... fuzzy." Devon rubbed the back of his neck. If they didn't do anything, why didn't Devon go home instead?

"Ah, right." Connor ducked out of the room and reappeared moments later with a tray filled with waffles and potatoes and several glasses of water. "You should probably eat this. I wasn't sure how hungover you'd be this morning."

"I'm not that hungover." Devon glanced away, his lip jutting out a bit.

"Eat anyways." Connor brought the tray to the nightstand next to Devon and sat down. "You must be hungry, you've been sleeping for almost 12 hours."

"12 hours? Isn't it morning?" Devon reached over to the tray and picked up a piece of toast and started nibbling on it.

Connor shook his head. "Not anymore, it's after 1 o'clock."

"What?" Devon rubbed the side of his temples. He was mostly asleep and slowly processing words. "So you've been sitting around all morning? Don't tell me you were watching me sleep…"

"It's Thursday, I should've gone to the office." Connor said calmly. At least he wasn't rushing Devon out of his place, but Devon still gave him a weird look. "I've been working from home this morning."

"Shit, I guess I'm late for work too then…" he groaned and leaned back against the

53

pillows. "I don't wanna go!" He pulled the covers up to below his chin, staying curled up.

"Stay and eat, I can take you to the cafe." Connor snatched a piece of Devon's potatoes as Devon swatted his hand away from his food.

"How far are you from the cafe?" Devon mumbled, reaching for another piece of his breakfast, only his arm extending from his blanket cocoon. "Don't you have to work?"

"I'll be going into the office anyways. It's all still downtown." Connor stood up and went to the window. He drew back the curtains. "This is the view."

Devon sat up and looked out the window, he could see all of the city. Devon knew exactly where he was now. It was that new apartment building in the nice end of downtown. It was officially the tallest building in Mount Oolie. The cheapest apartment in the building would cost Devon two months of his pay. They had to be almost on the top floor to get a view like this. "You must do well for yourself. Owning a restaurant, living in the nicest place in Mount Oolie…"

Connor chuckled and went back to the bed and sat next to Devon. "I invest in Rose Gold, I own a startup. But I do like being able to live here. Does it make you shy?"

"No." Devon shrunk back against the pillows. Of course it made him shy, or at the least embarrassed since he felt like such a commoner next to this prince of a man. He picked up the tray and set it in his lap, trying to use it as an excuse to scoot away from Connor. "You're awfully cozy…"

Connor smiled. "So are you." Devon stared at him, his brow furrowed. Connor shrugged. "At least you were last night."

"I'm not much of a cuddler…" Devon looked back down at his tray.

"We didn't cuddle. But you were very affectionate." Connor let out a sigh. "I didn't think it was just the alcohol."

"It's only been one date…" Devon mumbled as Connor snuck another piece of Devon's potatoes. Devon swatted at his hand again. "Why didn't you get some for yourself when you got this for me?"

"Because I already ate what I made," Connor said with a chuckle.

Made? Devon looked down at the tray. The food looked too good to be homemade, every dish had a perfect presentation. "Nah, you totally picked this up."

"Are you assuming I can't cook because I'm an alpha?" Connor tilted his head to the side.

That hadn't crossed Devon's mind, but now that Connor said it, his face turned pink. "Fine, fine, you can cook decent food."

"Just decent?" Connor let out a melodramatic sigh. "And here I thought making you breakfast would impress you."

"Yeah well…" Devon took a bite and swallowed. It was definitely more delicious than just decent. He did remember kissing Connor and liking it. Maybe Connor wasn't so bad. He leaned over and kissed Connor's cheek. "Thanks."

Connor grinned, leaning over to peck Devon's lips. Devon didn't think he'd get so affectionate so fast, the alcohol had taken away so many of his reservations last night. But there was no alcohol this morning and these kisses were still a bit awkward to him. Or maybe Connor seemed to be freely taking as many kisses as he wanted. He turned red and looked away as he shoved a large bite of food in his mouth.

Connor chuckled and sat next to Devon, wrapping his arm around Devon's shoulders. Devon furrowed his brow as he kept eating. Wasn't Connor a bit too close so soon? This was still technically their first date. Despite what Connor said, he didn't remember all of this affection and he wasn't ready for it now. He quickly finished what was left on the tray and wiped his mouth with the back of his hand despite there being a napkin on the tray. "I should probably get going."

"I'll walk you there."

"If it's walking distance, I can go myself." Devon scrunched his shoulders. He didn't move away from Connor, but he didn't exactly settle in either.

Connor kept his arm around Devon's shoulders though. "My office isn't far from the cafe. I'll go with you."

"Okay…" Devon flung the covers off and stepped out of bed. He had to admit that was the comfiest bed he'd ever slept in. "Where did you sleep last night?"

"My room." Connor looked up at Devon, leaning forward to rest his elbow on his thigh.

"P r e p a r e d with a t w o - b e d r o o m penthouse…" Devon shoved his hands in his pants pockets. "I'm not your first *guest*, am I?" Connor's silence answered the question for him. It was one date, Devon had no right to feel jealous. But he felt it deep in his gut. "I really should go."

Connor stood up, picking up Devon's hoodie from the end of the bed for him. Devon snagged his phone from the bedside table and shoved it in his pants pocket as he walked out of the room. Connor quietly followed him and led him to the front door. It was such a strange sensation, Devon didn't really remember this apartment at all. Just how much had he had to drink? It looked familiar, but that was about it.

Even as they both left the apartment and rode the elevator down to the lobby, Devon didn't say a word. He didn't mean to punish Connor. He just wasn't ready for the sudden step forward he and Connor had taken.

As they walked down the streets, Devon took a glance at Connor. There was such sadness in the way he stared straight ahead and kept his hands at his sides without looking towards Devon at all. Devon let out a long sigh, knowing that he'd made things awkward for the redhead. He glanced away as he snuck his hand down to hold Connor's.

Connor finally did look over at Devon and smiled. He held Devon's hand back tightly. He glanced back to the redhead to see that smile. He quickly looked away again, his face totally red. He didn't say anything, but kept holding Connor's hand. He did want a second date, but maybe one where he'd be more conscious about the decisions he makes.

The rest of the walk went by quickly and, soon enough, they were standing in front of Almond Blossom Tea. Connor stopped and stepped closer to Devon. Devon was still a bright shade of red, but he didn't back away.

"Let's go out again soon." Connor grinned.

Devon nodded, still avoiding eye contact. "I'll text you, promise."

"If you don't, I'll be back for another boba." Connor chuckled.

"You should come get one anyways." Devon bit his lower lip.

"Then maybe I will stop by later."

Devon nodded and quickly kissed Connor's cheek before dashing inside the cafe. His face was still red, but he tried to hide it by zipping his hoodie all the way up and bringing the hood close around his neck. He wasn't really looking up at the cafe, hoping he could sneak into the employee room without being noticed.

"You're actually here?"

Devon stopped right in his tracks, that was not the usual derisive comment from Robbie. He turned to see Kieran leaning against the counter, arms folded over his chest.

"I'm not that late." Devon shoved his hands in his pockets. "You don't usually care."

Kieran stood up straight and walked up to Devon. "I care when the son of my good friend disappears and so she comes to me, asking if he's working late and is in tears when we both realize that we don't know where he is or who he's with and he's not responding to his phone."

"I'm an adult." Devon tried to walk past Kieran, into the employee room.

But Kieran followed him right in and closed the door behind them. "I don't care if you're an adult. It's not about being an adult or not, it's about treating the people who care about you with respect."

"I respect my mom!" Devon whipped around to face him.

"Really? Then at least tell her that you were going to be late! She's been worrying about you all night and I had to do my best to convince her to wait before filing a missing person's report!"

Devon shrugged. "You didn't need to do that. I wasn't gone that long."

"You know what, I hired you because your mom asked for help with you." Kieran took a step forward and shook his head. "I owed her big time, she could've asked me for anything and I would've done it for her, but she asked me to help you. This is who you're disrespecting."

"I…" Devon leaned against the wall by the coat rack and crossed his arms over his chest. "Not like I meant to be thoughtless…"

Kieran let out a long breath and slowly walked over to Devon. "Your mom hoped I could help you with more than just a job. Being an omega is hard."

"You do seem to employ a lot of us…" He thought of himself and Robbie, he wasn't even sure if Kieran had any other help.

Kieran tilted his head to the side, raising a brow. "Do I blend in that well to you?"

"Huh?" Devon looked right at Kieran.

"I don't just employ omegas, I am one."

Devon blinked a few times, not really believing it, but also it somehow made sense. He'd never given it much thought before. Kieran was his boss, so didn't it make more sense for him to be an alpha or at least a beta?

Kieran shrugged. "This town is weird. It's got a mix of traditional people who think we all have to fit into a mold. Then there's also those modernists that say we aren't bound by our type, but still put other people into those same guidelines." Devon scrunched his shoulders together, avoiding eye contact. Kieran let out a breath. "I know how difficult it can be. Especially for omegas like us."

Devon balled his hands into fists. He did not need to be lectured on being an omega. He kept most of his struggles to himself, at least the ones relating to his type.

"I'm always here if you need to talk about anything."

Devon pushed himself off the wall and shouldered past Kieran. He whipped around to look at him. "Honestly, you don't know how difficult things have been for me, so don't act like you know. You live in Mount Oolie where everything seems like a fairytale and everyone gets a goddamn happy ending. Mount Oolie is known for making omegas like us and everyone expects us to be something special. As if we're some sort of prize. Outside of this place... hell, even being back here, people are traditional everywhere and just want what they want and don't give a shit about you! So don't act like you give a shit about me. You may care about my mom, but I'm not even worth having around as an employee!"

Kieran could only stare back at Devon, mouth agape. Devon spun around on his heel and stalked out of the room. He walked out of the cafe entirely, not giving a shit if he was supposed to be working. His feet carried him down the streets, he hardly paid attention to where he was going until he was walking by the old man's house at the end of the Tree Streets neighborhood.

"Fuck..." He didn't want to go home, but his feet seemed to carry him there.

He turned around, but a familiar voice came from behind him. "Devon?" He stopped without thinking about it. "Devon! I'm so glad I found you!" Mark's voice sounded closer this time.

Devon let out a breath and turned around. "Mr. Waller…"

"I've been looking for you all night!" Mark stood next to him and put his hand on Devon's back. Devon flinched but didn't pull away, even though Mark was walking him back to his mom's house. Mark stopped when they were on the sidewalk in front of the house. "You know… your mom is really worried about you."

Devon nodded. "I'll go talk to her."

Mark nodded and took a step back. Devon waited for a moment, hoping that Mark would go back to whatever he was doing, but it seemed that he was sticking around. Devon took a few steps towards the front door, still feeling the gaze on his back. He let out a breath and walked up to the door. He opened it slightly, and only then did Mark walk away.

Devon walked inside. "Mom?"

He heard something being knocked over in the living room, but before Devon could even go see what happened, his mom ran from that very room and right up to him. She hugged him tightly without saying a word. He let out a breath and looked down. He hugged her back, feeling very guilty for not checking his phone last night. "I'm sorry."

"Don't disappear again."

"I won't."

CHAPTER 8

Connor happily strolled up to his building, getting there right as a group of employees from his office were walking in. He jogged a few steps and caught the door behind them. A couple of the employees smiled and chatted a bit until they saw him. Practically all of them quietly waited for the elevator, shifting from foot to foot. One employee dared to smile back and asked, "Was there a good lunch meeting?"

Connor felt bad that he didn't know the person's name. He returned the smile and nodded. "Something like that."

Once in the elevator, everyone was silent until the doors opened on their floor. Connor was the first one out of the elevator and even went to hold the office door open for everyone else. A few people blinked and looked at each other. Was this behavior so uncommon for him? Well, he had been pretty sullen the last three months or so since Zach left. But he didn't want to think about that.

He walked in last, going right to his office. He knew he didn't usually work from home, but it was worth it. All of his morning tasks were easily done on his laptop and his afternoon meetings didn't start for another 15 minutes. Sammy stopped him at the door, blocking his view. "There seems to be an issue…"

"Issue?" That was not the first word he wanted to hear back in the office.

"About your meeting with Kameron…" Sammy rubbed the back of his neck. "It would seem that the engineers have made their own time to talk to you."

Connor furrowed his brow. He didn't mind meeting with employees when he had the time, but now was not the time. He needed the update on the development of their product. If it had been just one engineer, he would be inclined to say they should reschedule. "All of the engineers?" Connor had to clarify.

Sammy nodded. "All of them that report directly to Kameron."

All of them… that was not a good sign. He let out a long breath, trying to hold onto the good feeling he'd had from being with Devon. "Alright, I'll talk to them, what meeting room are they in?" Sammy glanced at his office. Connor let out a short, frustrated breath. "We need to have a talk after this. Get Meeting Room A cleared now."

The company was still growing and the entire office space only took up one floor of the building. There weren't many meeting rooms, so Connor had been used to sharing and scheduling them alongside his employees, but his office was different. His office, though it was fairly small, was his one space that he did not share and only had a select few in for meetings there. Was this what he got for having an omega as his assistant? He didn't want to judge someone based on their type and he'd no major problems with Sammy before, but he couldn't let his assistant get bullied by the other employees.

Connor swung the door to his office open. The group of engineers standing on the other side all stopped murmuring and looked at him. Connor held the door open and stepped back and to the side. "Meet me in Meeting Room A." At first, no one moved and Connor was losing his patience. He glared at them. "Now."

The first engineer to move was one standing towards the back of the group with his shoulders scrunched together. He looked quite different from the rest of the engineers who were pushing their shoulders back unnecessarily. It seemed odd that this meek person would lead the group in leaving, but rather it seemed more likely that he was more intimidated by Connor than the engineers around him. Either way, it got the group moving. Connor didn't go directly to the meeting room himself though. He went into his office and set his things down on his desk. He took a breath, savoring the moment alone. If he thought hard enough, he could still smell the scent of honey in Devon's hair.

Connor walked back out of his office. Sammy scrunched his shoulders and ducked his head down close to his computer, staring at the calendar he had pulled open. Connor shook his head. He wasn't going to fire Sammy, but he did have to have a serious conversation with him. He continued to the meeting room and opened the door. Once again, the murmuring stopped as soon as he entered.

He took a seat at the head of the table and looked around at the 5 engineers before him. He leaned back and looked at each of them. "Alright, let's get started. It would seem that you've gone past my assistant to get time on my calendar and barge into my office. I hope that what you want to discuss is important."

The meek engineer scrunched his shoulders together more and shrunk back against the chair. The other three in the room looked to the man sitting to Connor's right. The man sat up tall with broad shoulders and a grimace on his face that didn't seem to change even when he spoke. If he wasn't mistaken, this man was named Matt. "We want to talk to you about Kameron."

Connor looked the man in the eye as he crossed one foot over his opposite knee. "Regarding?"

"His leadership. He's making questionable choices and refuses to let any of us work. Which means our own subordinates don't get the proper work to do." Matt rested his hand on the table, trying to be more relaxed, but to Connor, it looked like a fake gesture to lure him into buying Matt's story. But Connor wasn't going to fall for a cheap power play.

"You don't have subordinates, you have individual contributors. What questionable choices?" Connor urged him to elaborate. If there was a genuine concern, then he knew it had to be looked into. But Kameron was a man he'd personally picked for the role. He didn't have the same history with him as he did with Riley, but Kameron was a young up-and-comer from Mount Oolie. If Connor wasn't mistaken, no one in the room except himself was from Mount Oolie.

"Regarding the tech stack. We'll quickly be surpassed by our competitors at this rate." Matt pushed his shoulders back and lightly hit his fist against the table as he spoke, "This small-town kid doesn't know—"

Connor raised his hand. Matt fell silent. "Small-town kid?" The whole room was silent in response. No one dared answer Connor.

Connor sat up straight and pulled his chair to the table. "Tell me, does Kameron make questionable choices because he's younger than you or is it because he's from a 'small town'?"

"Sir," Matt spoke slowly, "that's not what I meant—"

"Then what did you mean?" Connor looked Matt right in the eyes. "Surely, you didn't mean to look down on this small town that our office is located in? Kameron calls this place home, and so do I. Is that a problem?"

One of the other engineers in the room finally spoke up, "We're concerned about the company's future." Connor turned to look at her. She gulped, but stood her ground. "We're not able to make efficient progress and left unchecked, we could see very negative results."

"Then this is something I will look into myself." Connor looked at the group of them. "It's not up to you to go over Kameron's head to try and have him replaced."

"W-we weren't trying to do that!" The meek engineer spoke up. Try as he might, it seemed that Connor had forgotten his name or never learned it in the first place. This engineer didn't seem like the kind of person who would be introducing himself to the CEO of the company he works for.

"Is that so?"

"Of course not." Matt spoke up. He smiled at Connor, but looked over to the meek man and shot him a glare. Connor saw it and thought perhaps that was exactly what Matt wanted—to be the new CTO. That wouldn't happen as long as Connor could help it. He didn't need an executive who would disrespect him.

Connor stood up. "Then I'll end this meeting for now."

Matt nodded and was the first one out of the room. The others followed after, but Connor stopped the meek man by the door. He really did feel bad for not knowing who he was. "What's your name?"

The man bit his lip and took a step back, his back hitting the door frame. "Please don't fire me. I didn't want to join this meeting, but the others... they said—"

"I won't fire you." Connor stopped the omega's rambling. Now that he was standing close enough, he could smell it on him. "What's your name?"

"Tyler..." the redhead omega looked down, shoving his hands in his pockets.

"Tyler, you seemed to disagree with Matt in there, what do you think about Kameron?"

"I think he's good at what he does. I dunno, I just... I think Matt lives and breathes work, like maybe he needs to just get laid once in a while." Tyler looked off to the side, thinking as he spoke.

Connor stared at him, surprised to hear that coming from someone who'd been so shy to say more than two words in front of him.

Tyler's eyes widened. "Oh my god!" He covered his face with his hands. "I didn't mean! I just! Please don't tell anyone I said that!"

Connor laughed and nodded. "Don't worry, I won't. Thank you for speaking up today, Tyler."

He nodded and quickly ducked out of the meeting room and darted back to his desk.

Connor shook his head to himself and walked back to his office. "Sammy, change my meeting with Kameron to tomorrow and give him all morning." Sammy nodded. Connor was about to close his office door behind him, but he turned back to his assistant one more time. "Oh and Sammy? Never let Matt or any of the other employees barge past you. No one comes into my office when I'm not here. No one."

● ● ●

Connor was in the kitchen of Rose Gold with Tristan, looking at his phone in his hands.

Even though they'd gone on a date and Devon spent the night with him, he still didn't have Devon's number because he never texted him back. That did not make Connor happy. Tristan came over with a plate, adding the garnish. He looked up to Connor, furrowing his brow. "If you're just going to stand there, maybe you should get out of my kitchen?"

"Hey, shouldn't I have access to be back here?" Connor complained.

"Sure, but you're in the way and you're not even saying anything." Tristan had virtually no patience. He handed the plate to a sous chef who put the dish out for the waiters. "It's the middle of the dinner rush, so I'm a bit busy."

"That's why I thought being quiet would be better." Connor rolled his eyes.

"But I can smell your glowering all the way from across the kitchen." Tristan took a breath and stopped what he was doing, letting the rest of the kitchen staff handle the orders. "What's wrong? You only come back here when something's wrong or when something's great and, clearly, it's not the latter."

Connor let out a long breath. He was easily readable by one of his oldest friends. "He was supposed to text me by now. We came here for dinner, I took him back to my place—"

"Woah! On the first date?" Tristan blinked at him a few times. "Isn't that a little... indecent?"

Connor scrunched his brow and tilted his head to the side. "Isn't that old fashioned of you?"

"I guess I still think that two or three dates should be the minimum before you sleep with someone."

Connor shook his head. "It wasn't like that. He was too drunk to tell me where he lived and so I thought it would be better to take him home."

"And you weren't tempted to...?" Tristan leaned in, speaking hushedly.

"No, what kind of alpha do you think I am?" Though if Connor were to speak candidly, he was tempted to do things with Devon. Omegas' pheromones were always stronger when they were uninhibited, and Devon's scent was sweet as honey.

"If you weren't tempted then maybe he's not meant for you? Sometimes people's scents don't match, that's how you know you're not supposed to mate someone." Tristan shrugged and leaned against the counter, leaving his cooking for someone else to finish.

Connor shook his head and let out a nervous laugh. "That definitely isn't the case... I could smell him and oh did he smell good..."

Connor wasn't even looking at his phone anymore, he didn't notice the message that came in.

Tristan elbowed him in the side. "You were tempted! Don't act so well mannered!"

"I'm not going to do something while he's drunk!"

"But that's not the same as being tempted. It's natural for alphas to be tempted, doesn't mean you should act on those temptations." Tristan shook his head and laughed a bit.

"Okay, I was tempted." Connor folded his arms over his chest. "He smelled so good, I mean *good*."

"Better than Zach?" Tristan said tentatively.

Connor nodded, not really registering that he was talking about his ex. "Way better. It was so sweet and he smelled like honey. Do you think it's from the cafe? Or is it just him?"

Tristan shrugged and stared off into space. "Dunno. They say that you can really only identify someone's scent if they're your destined mate."

"Destined mate... I wonder if it is like that with him, I didn't think it would be that easy to find a destined mate."

"Was it easy to find him though?" Tristan looked at Connor.

"I mean, I wasn't even looking and I found him." Connor smiled to himself, this notion gave him a new hope. He looked at his phone again to see if Devon had texted him and there was a message from a number not in his contacts. It read: "Hey Connor"

Connor quickly sent a message back, "Devon?"

The response was slow, but Connor could see the typing icon on the screen and left his phone open as he waited. Tristan leaned over his shoulder to look. "Is it him?"

"I hope so." They both waited until finally another text came in: "Yeah"

Connor chuckled to himself. Devon sure didn't seem to be a big texter. Then he'd have to do something better. "Let's go on another date."

"Uh…" that response confused him. And it was another minute or so before Devon sent another. "In a week?"

"Okay. How about we do a picnic?"

No sooner had Connor sent the message then Tristan looked at him, rolling his eyes. "A picnic? Really?"

"He might like it, okay?" Connor looked down at his phone, waiting to see if Devon would indeed like the suggestion.

It took a few more minutes, but Devon finally responded: "Sure, sounds good"

"See?" Connor showed Tristan the message.

Tristan furrowed his brow. "He doesn't sound that enthusiastic though."

"I don't think he's really a big texter." Connor shrugged. "We're going on another date and you're not going to ruin my mood."

"Then maybe you can stop ruining the mood of my kitchen now?" Tristan chuckled.

CHAPTER 9

Devon closed the messages on his phone and tossed it to the side of his bed. He didn't want to wait so long to see Connor again, but after last night… he was sure his mom would not be pleased with him making plans again. Once she had finally pulled back from hugging him, she immediately started yelling at him. Devon did his best to remind himself that it was just because she was worried. After all, Kieran had basically warned him about as much.

He promised her that he would at least let her know his plans if he had any. Not that she could, but if she could, she would've grounded him. He knew that seeing anyone or even going to work would have to wait. This was a problem of working for someone his mom knew, Kieran would think that spending time with his mom was a reasonable excuse from working. But Devon wanted to use work as an excuse to get out of the house. He wasn't committed enough to his plan to even make it work, so he voluntarily stayed home.

"Devi! Dinner time!" His mom called out to him.

He let out a long breath, not really wanting to go downstairs and eat. After skipping work, he'd hardly done anything today except sleep. He'd heard his mom make a phone call to Kieran and that was it. Did she even have the day off? He figured she had to have since she'd been looking for him since last night. He certainly felt bad about it, but it wasn't like anything bad happened.

He let out a long sigh and stood up from his bed. He stretched and looked at his phone again. He hoped Connor wouldn't get bored waiting for him. A guy like that, there had to be a ton of omegas lined up, wanting to date him. Why Connor ever wanted him, some bumbling barista… was beyond him.

He took his phone with him as he walked downstairs. "Thanks, Mom."

She smiled and nodded. "Of course, Devi."

He scratched the back of his head. Maybe he shouldn't ask, but he had to, "Was it okay for you to miss work today?"

"Never you mind," was all she said. Devon knew she was holding back.

He stared at the food she put on the table and he slowly sat down. He couldn't look up at her. "You didn't have to take the day off."

"Then don't disappear again so I won't have to use up all my sick days." She said so matter of factly. That was really the response that he'd been expecting.

"I won't, but…" Devon didn't want to tell her, but he couldn't have her find out any other way.

"But?" She looked right at him, brow furrowed.

"I will see him again." He mumbled, "Just so you know…"

"Are you sure about that?" Neither of them touched their food.

"He was nice, I think I should." Devon shrugged and used a fork to push the vegetables around his plate.

"You don't owe him anything for being nice." She leaned over the table, towards him. "You don't have to do anything."

He shook his head. "I know. I want to." But did he want to? Or was he doing it because Connor wanted to? Or because he could use it as an excuse to get out of the house? Well, he wouldn't question his own motives, at least not for now.

She nodded slowly. "I still think you should wait and see." She started to eat slowly.

Devon knew that waiting wasn't an option with such a prolific alpha. But he wasn't going to start a debate with his mom. He started to eat too. She'd made his favorite, from-scratch ravioli, and it actually did make him smile. "This must've taken you all day to make."

"I'm happy to do it." She smiled back.

"Thank you." He took a big bite. He did love the food and he knew that his mom would appreciate being appreciated, so he wanted to fully enjoy the meal that she put such effort into making.

Both of them ate in silence. He didn't know what to say and she seemed to feel the same way. When his plate was finished, he stood up and took the plate with him to the kitchen. He walked back to the dining table to see his mom staring at him. He glanced away. "Should I bother going to work tomorrow?"

"It's up to you," she said and held her breath.

He hated it when she said things like that. He knew there was a right or wrong answer to things like that even if it didn't seem like there should be. He shrugged and shook his head. "I don't have to."

"Okay, Devon, then I'll bring us home something special for dinner." She smiled and nodded.

He nodded back. At least he chose right for his own response. "I'm gonna go upstairs, I think." To do what, he didn't know, but he just felt like being alone.

She nodded. "I'll be here if you want to play a game or watch a show together."

She had to say that. Now he felt bad for going off to his own room. "Maybe in a bit." Before she could say anything else, he walked up to his room and took his phone out again. No notifications… He wished Connor would text him again or something…

● ● ●

A week later, Devon was serving boba at Almond Blossom Tea again. It felt weird though since he was there in the morning. After missing so many days, Kieran had requested he come in for a whole day so Robbie could take the day off. Devon wasn't too happy about doing anything for the blonde, but he wasn't going to say no to Kieran. So he was standing at the register, taking orders. Luckily, it was a slow day.

Devon leaned against the counter as Kieran handed out the last order in their queue. "Why did I have to be here in the morning? Robbie never comes in the mornings."

Kieran let out a long breath. "Do you have to be so petulant?"

"Maybe I do!" He really didn't like being called out. Maybe he could take a chill pill, but it was still a valid question.

"I used to want kids, but if they're going to turn out as argumentative as you…"

"Fuck you." Devon glared at his boss. He didn't even say anything that bad. Yet. "Aren't you too old to have kids?"

"Just how old do you think I am?!" Kieran stood up straight. "I could fire you, you know."

"You haven't yet. I tried for the first two weeks I started working here." Devon shrugged. He'd given up on getting fired.

"Then maybe I'll make you work more morning shifts."

"You wouldn't!"

"Try me." Kieran glared back. "Not that it's any of your business, but I'm not even 30."

"So old." Devon stuck his tongue out.

"And that alpha you're going on a date with?" Kieran put his hands on his hips. "Isn't he over 30?"

Well, Kieran had him there. Connor certainly seemed more mature, though Devon didn't know his exact age. "I'm not a teenager either."

"You act like one." Kieran started to make two drinks.

"Who are those for?"

"Me and you unless you ask me one more stupid question."

Devon was quiet for a moment. He did want the drink… Kieran was making strawberry milk tea with boba, his favorite. He patiently waited for Kieran to finish before saying anything else. When Kieran handed him the drink, he stabbed a straw through the lid and took a long sip. "I can't make it the way you do…"

"Then I'll show you how I make it next time." Kieran smiled and relaxed a bit.

The drink really hit the spot for Devon since he had been getting hungry. He looked down at his drink. "Can you tell my mom that I'll be out again late tonight?"

"Why do I have to tell her?" Kieran furrowed his brow, taking a long slurp from the drink.

"She'd be too disappointed to hear it from me. I don't think she wants me to see that guy again." But tonight was finally the night that they were going to go out again.

"I don't think she sees it like that."

"I know she's not happy about it since I didn't tell her about it before. I'd rather just not say anything." He didn't tell her anything about Connor, not even his name. He knew it wasn't a good idea to keep things from his mom, but what was he supposed to do? If she knew that he was ten years older than him, surely she'd make him stop seeing him?

Kieran shook his head. "I'll tell her if she comes looking for you. But you should tell her yourself first."

CHAPTER 10

Connor sat back in his desk chair, waiting for Kameron. They'd talked at length after Matt and the other engineers had come to him. As expected, Kameron had gotten angry and dug his own heels in. Needless to say, in the last week, their engineering progress had been virtually nonexistent.

Through the glass door to his office, he saw Matt shoulder his way past Sammy and knock on the door. Connor took a deep breath, trying to restrain himself from biting off Matt's head. He motioned for the engineer to come in. "Yes?"

"I know Kameron has been having a lot of meetings with you. I'm just wondering when we can get an update on what will happen with him," Matt said without even closing the door behind him.

Such an act of disrespect did not go unnoticed by Connor, especially since Kameron was walking up and surely would've heard. Connor shrugged. "I will do what I see fit. In the meantime, I suggest you continue to do the job that you're paid for."

Matt clenched his jaw and forced a smile. "Yes, sir." He stepped out of the office.

Kameron gave Matt a glare, and Connor assumed it to be mutual. Kameron walked into Connor's office and he did shut the door behind him. "Should I ask why he was here?"

"It wouldn't be right for me to say, but I'm sure you can imagine the reason." Connor nodded. The reason had been the same for the whole week. He really wanted this to be over. "Take a seat. I want this hold up with our product ended."

Kameron sat across from Connor. "I would love that too. I won't say that the engineers can't do what you're asking for, but that they don't want to."

"I don't even understand why everyone is so personally up in arms over this. What happened to people's work ethic?" Connor couldn't stop himself from letting some of his true feelings out. "I know you've described what needs to be done and I will admit that I've run the same ideas by Matt and he laughed at it."

"He's never brought up such a disagreement with me." Kameron frowned. "None of the engineers have."

"I think most of them are following Matt on this. Or so it seems that way from when they insisted on speaking with me." Connor rubbed his temples with his fingers.

"You know… I'm not sure what to do about him." Kameron leaned back in his seat. "I know you were the one who found me for this job and I love it. I don't want to hand over this tech to anyone else, but are we going to keep being met with this kind of obstacle?"

Connor shook his head. "I've been giving it a lot of thought and I don't think it's the technology at all. Everything is doable. The problem is who we've hired to follow through."

"I know they can do it though." Kameron was still defending the engineers that turned their backs on him.

"That doesn't matter if they won't do it." Connor shook his head. "I think it's time to start the termination process with Matt and possibly others of your direct-reports."

"Hiring new people to replace them might make the progress slower."

"In the short term, but I do not take kindly to giving out paychecks to people who don't work."

"All of my reports? Some of them have teams of their own, the teams might find it demotivating if they lose their own managers."

"Keep some. I know Tyler wouldn't follow the path Matt has chosen." Connor thought about it, Tyler was the only engineer that he didn't currently dislike. After that meeting, Connor had been keeping a close eye on Kameron and all of his reports.

"Too bad he doesn't have his own team." Kameron let out a short breath.

"Maybe it's time he did." Connor thought for a moment.

"Really?" Kameron furrowed his brow and leaned forward. "I don't mean to be… traditional, but he's not an alpha."

"Matt is, we can see how well that turned out."

"I definitely think Tyler is a better employee than Matt, but a better leader? I don't know." Kameron leaned back. "It's just that he's far more… typical."

"Matt said you were a small-town kid." Connor pointed out.

Kameron sat up straight. "That f—" Kameron stopped himself before losing it in front of the CEO.

Connor chuckled. "We aren't always what we seem to each other. I think it's better to give Tyler the chance, especially since we'll need someone to take over Matt's team."

"Matt has the biggest team, this won't be easy." Kameron swallowed.

"You can handle it. And if you can't, then did I hire the right person for your job?" Connor chuckled.

"Don't worry about that, I'll definitely follow through." Kameron nodded.

"Good." Connor nodded. He looked down at his watch. That had taken up most of his morning, on the bright side, that meant that he was closer to seeing Devon again after work today and he was so excited to see him again. The week had gone by too slowly, yet at the same time been filled with too much stress.

● ● ●

Connor walked up to the cafe, smiling when he saw Devon through the window. He noticed that a different person was working with Devon. For a moment, he wondered what happened to the blonde. He walked inside and got in the line. He slowly moved forward until it was his turn to order.

"How can I help—" Devon stopped as he looked up and saw Connor.

Connor grinned. "I know I'm early, but I didn't want to wait any longer." He really did feel the week melting away when he saw Devon's soft face. "How about you get me whatever your favorite drink is and I'll wait at a table until you're done?"

Devon nodded slowly, a small smile spreading over his lips. "One strawberry milk tea, coming up."

He smiled back and paid for the drink. He stepped back and waited for his drink. The other employee had been making most of the drinks for the customers, but Devon walked away from the register to make this one himself. Of course, that did not please the customer in line behind Connor. The other employee let out a sigh and took Devon's place at the register.

Connor watched intently, following Devon's every move. He seemed to know what he was doing a lot more now compared to the first time Connor saw him here. It wasn't long before Devon held out a creamy pink drink with chunks of strawberry and dark tapioca to Connor. Connor took it and, without even taking a sip, said, "It's even better than last time."

Devon raised a brow and let out a short huff. "At least try it first."

"I will, I will." Connor chuckled and put a straw through the lid. He took a sip. "I was right. It's delicious."

Devon grinned back at him. "I'll be ready soon."

Connor nodded and leaned over the counter to kiss his cheek. "I'll be here."

Connor went to sit at one of the few empty tables. Most people took their drinks and left, not sticking around to sit for a while. But most of the tables were occupied by people studying and chatting and Connor was lucky to claim one of the few tables left. He took his time to sip his drink, it seemed like Devon might be busy for a while. He had gotten here over an hour before the cafe closed after all. He kept glancing at Devon. He seemed to have more pep in his step and smiled at the customers more. Connor knew it was better for service, but he still felt a twinge every time Devon smiled so sincerely at someone else. Connor swallowed down the feeling, no use giving in to any jealousy.

After a while, Devon had a quick conversation with the other man behind the counter and the man nodded. Connor tilted his head to the side, wondering what it was all about when Devon disappeared into the back room. But Devon reappeared moments later and walked up to Connor's table. "I can leave a bit early today."

Connor grinned and stood up. "Really? It'll be okay?"

Devon nodded. "Yeah, my boss knows I have evening plans."

Connor extended his hand to Devon. "Then let's go. I hope you don't mind stopping at my place first. I didn't want to let the food spoil while I was at work."

Devon looked at his hand for a minute, but nodded slowly and took his hand. Connor gave it a gentle squeeze. Devon looked up at him. "I was thinking, it would be nice to have a cozy dinner at home too."

Connor smirked and tilted his head to the side. He was trying really hard to not read too much into the request, but all he was thinking of was different ways Devon would look good naked... He nodded and started to walk. "Sure, we can stay at my place. It'll make the food even fresher."

"I'm happy to eat whatever you made," Devon's voice was quiet but the sentiment was sincere.

"Are you?" Connor chuckled. "Well, you did seem to enjoy my cooking last week. I hope you enjoy this just as much."

They both walked quietly to Connor's apartment building. Devon was looking all around, taking in the sight. Connor did notice that Devon was far more present this time than the last time he brought him here. Before, although it had been alluring, Devon had been leaning heavily against Connor and staring at him more than anything around him. As much as Connor did love that kind of attention from

Devon, seeing this genuine amazement in Devon's eyes was just as worth it.

He led them up to his penthouse and opened the door for Devon. Devon walked in quickly and spun around as he looked at the spacious apartment. He went right to the large windows on the opposite side of the room. "Do you ever get sick from looking down at this height?" Devon pressed his face against the glass, looking down. "I don't feel so good…"

Connor furrowed his brow. He wasn't exactly meaning for his apartment to be an amusement park for Devon. He walked over to Devon and rested a hand on his shoulder. "No, but I also don't stare down like that."

Devon leaned back and looked up at Connor. "Sorry, I just… I've never been up this high in a building before." Connor chuckled and Devon blushed. "Well, not that I can remember as clearly…"

"Do you want a tour?" Connor chuckled. He would do it if Devon wanted to, but he would rather not.

Devon shook his head. "Just to know where the bathroom is."

Connor nodded and led Devon away from the window. He showed him down a hall that had been by the guest bedroom Devon had used before. He pointed to a door on the left. "Right in there. I'll be in the kitchen."

Devon nodded and disappeared into the bathroom. Connor went back to the kitchen and got out the sliced fruit and vegetables he'd prepared for the picnic and arranged them onto serving platters. He decided to make a different main course though. Sandwiches were perfect for a picnic, but this was more serious and Connor wanted to impress Devon. A part of him wondered why he didn't suggest this in the first place? Maybe it was because of the way Devon didn't seem to want to get too close after the last time he was here. After all, having a cozy dinner in his apartment did feel like taking more than a few steps forward.

He got the food cooking on the stove and set the table. He got out his nice dishes and arranged everything neatly and properly on his table. Everything had to be just right, Connor wanted to see that amazed look in Devon's eyes again.

CHAPTER 11

Devon splashed his face with cool water, taking a deep breath as he straightened up in front of the bathroom sink. It did feel like things had escalated quickly with Connor and it was his own fault. He was the one who had suggested staying in! And made a fool of himself ogling Connor's apartment... He hadn't meant to act like such a child, but it really did feel so new to him. His mom did have a nice house, but it wasn't as nice as this.

He took another deep breath and pried his fingers from the edge of the sink. He snatched the towel from the rack and dried his face off. His shoulders sank as he held the towel to his face. Maybe the cool water would help him keep a level head? He felt a buzz against his side and pulled his phone out of his jacket pocket. There was a message from his mom. He gulped and looked away as he opened his phone. Maybe the message wouldn't be there when he opened his eyes. But it was. It read: "Kieran said that you might be late tonight?"

He swallowed, feeling bad that he hadn't texted her himself after all. If Kieran had told her, she didn't need to say anything, did she?

Saying something was only eating away at him. He should be home instead of in this posh apartment with this sexy guy he didn't have a chance with... He quickly sent a message. "I'm on a date. I'll be home soon." He shoved his phone back into his pocket, not wanting to see what his mom might send in response. Connor would probably be sending him home soon anyways. Devon had no place being here.

Devon took one more deep breath to get control himself. No need to make more of a fool of himself. He walked out of the bathroom and back the way Connor had brought him. He looked around. It seemed that Connor wasn't really into decorating. There wasn't much on the walls and the art that was there seemed to be surreal photography prints. It wasn't exactly Devon's go-to art, but it wasn't unattractive to him.

He stopped in the living room, realizing that he didn't know where the kitchen was. There were the large windows, where Devon had been staring out of moments ago, with the sectional couch facing them. Devon shuffled to the end of the couch, glancing around, not sure if he should go through the door on the far side of the room or not. He sat down on the edge of the dark blue couch and resisted the urge to take his phone back out and aimlessly scroll through notifications. He stared down at the zipper on his hoodie. Why did he have to wear something so basic for a date? Especially when Connor was looking handsome as ever in his button down shirt and slacks...

"You can make yourself comfortable." Devon looked up when he heard Connor's voice. Connor smiled as he walked out of the room on the far side. His sleeves were rolled up, strands of hair started to fall in front of his face, and he had a smudge of sauce on his cheek.

Devon gulped. He quickly looked away once he realized he was staring. He scratched his neck. "Sorry, I didn't mean to—" what was he even apologizing for? He didn't even know, he just felt the need to apologize for anything.

Connor shook his head and walked over. "I meant that you can take your jacket off if you'd like." He sat down next to Devon and smiled. Devon scooted over to make room for him and nearly fell off the couch, but caught himself just in time. Connor didn't seem to notice. "I decided to make something else, so the food will be a moment longer."

Devon nodded slowly. "Okay." He slowly took off his jacket. Some smell was making his head swim. Was it the delicious food or was it the delicious alpha sitting so close to him? He held his jacket in his lap, fiddling with the edges. It seemed to be the only way he could keep himself calm. Did Connor always smell like strawberry milk tea or was it just because he'd had that boba earlier?

A ding went off in the other room. "Ah, that'll be the food." Connor stood up and took a step away before looking back at Devon. "I won't be more than a minute."

Devon nodded, not saying a word. When he was alone again, he covered his face with his hands. What was he doing?! He shouldn't be here. He didn't belong in a place like this. If his past 'relationship' was any indicator, he wasn't the kind of person someone wanted to date… he wasn't even very good in bed, so why was he here? He stood up, taking a few steps towards the front door. But could he leave without saying anything? It would ruin any future he had with Connor. He wasn't ready to give that up. Connor was the best thing to happen to him in a while, even if dating Connor was a fantasy. He wanted that fantasy to last. He wanted to be held in Connor's strong arms. He wanted to be loved, even just for a moment.

His decision was made a moment later when Connor's voice came from behind him. "Have I made you uncomfortable?"

Devon shook his head without looking behind him. He clutched his jacket tighter. He heard Connor's footsteps against the wooden floor. His voice was so much closer now when he spoke, "Did I do something wrong?"

He could practically feel Connor's warm breath against the back of his neck. Those lips… Devon imagined how good it would feel to have them gently brushing against his skin. His knees felt weak, but he forced himself to keep standing. Connor's hand rested on his arm. "Please stay."

Devon couldn't resist any longer. He spun around in Connor's grip and took Connor's face in his hands. He kissed him deeply, using the kiss as a way to get his emotions out. All of his confusion, all of his desire, was in that passionate kiss. Connor's hands snuck around Devon's waist, pulling him closer. Devon didn't pull away from the kiss, instead he deepened it and went as far as to nibble on Connor's lower lip. He wasn't even sure if this is what he really wanted, but he didn't know how else to interpret the cloud in his mind. At least this way, he could focus on those tasty lips.

Connor forced himself back after a moment and looked into Devon's eyes. "Do you want to eat or…?"

Devon shook his head and kissed Connor again. He couldn't stop now, if he thought about what he was doing, he'd lose all of this confidence he built up in his mind. If Connor rather eat than kiss him… no, Devon wouldn't allow himself to go there. He pressed his body closer to Connor's, his own heart pounding between their chests. Connor pulled back once more, but didn't say a word. He took Devon by the wrist and led him to a room down the hall.

Connor threw open the bedroom door and pulled Devon inside. Devon's heart was racing as his gaze landed on the king-sized bed. The nerves started to build up and choke him again. But Connor kissed him again. Devon closed his eyes, letting those warm lips melt his heart and all the tension he was carrying. He readily kissed him back. The more they kissed, the more Devon smelled that strawberry milk tea. His head was filled with the delicious scent to the point where he felt lightheaded. It was easy enough for Connor to push him onto the soft, navy blue sheets and lay right over him. Devon couldn't think of anything except those lips.

He tugged at Connor's shirt, pulling it over his head. Connor was equally impatient with Devon's clothes and pulled them all off before kissing him again. Devon's face was a bright pink when he was completely naked in front of Connor. His own excitement was exposed and he couldn't hide anything from the alpha on top of him.

Connor's hands traveled over Devon's smooth skin, resting on his hips again. He started to grind their hips together. The friction of Connor's pants against Devon's bare skin was a little rough, but still arousing to Devon.

Connor parted from the kiss and then pulled Devon's legs apart. He licked his own fingers before rubbing them against Devon's entrance. The saliva covered fingers were cold and made Devon gasp in surprise. He covered his mouth with his hands after letting out such an embarrassing sound.

Connor slipped his fingers in, earning a low moan from the omega. Connor slowly moved his fingers in and out. "It's already wet down here."

Devon covered his face with his hands. He didn't need the alpha to point out how his body was reacting to being aroused. He was an omega and couldn't help it, his body was designed to take more than fingers.

Connor kissed Devon's hand over his face. He whispered, "You don't have to hide."

Oh, but Devon certainly felt like he did. Devon didn't take his hands away, all he did was shake his head. Now he was getting far too self-conscious and inadvertently tightened around Connor's fingers, making himself moan again.

Connor breathed against Devon's ear. "Show me your face."

Such sexy words, such a request, or was it more of a demand… regardless, Devon couldn't resist. He felt compelled to do as he was told. He slowly took his hands from his face and knotted his fingers in Connor's hair.

Connor looked right at him as he took his fingers out and exposed his own arousal. He kept eye contact as they connected. Devon's face was stained pink as he moaned from slowly being filled. Connor was certainly doing a lot to make him feel comfortable, but his heart was still pounding. He didn't mean to be so nervous, but he felt so exposed. "K-kiss me?"

Without another word, Connor leaned down and captured Devon's lips in a sweet kiss.

• • •

Devon rubbed his eyes and slowly opened them. He felt a warmth next to him and realized that he'd fallen asleep after they'd finished. His head was on Connor's chest and he slowly moved his head to look up at Connor. He was surprised to see that Connor was looking right back at him. His face turned a bright pink as he said, "D-did you sleep at all?"

Connor shook his head. "Not really, but it was nice to watch you sleep."

Devon hid his face against Connor's strong chest, which didn't help make him blush any less since Connor was quite fit, but at least Connor couldn't see it… "T-then you didn't have to stay!"

"I didn't have to, but I didn't want to wake you either." Connor ran his fingers through Devon's hair.

Those fingers made Devon feel so relaxed, but he didn't want to admit it and end up even more embarrassed. "Yeah, well…" He was definitely glad that Connor had stayed.

"It hasn't been that long." Connor chuckled. Devon didn't say anything in response, but scooted a little closer to him. He winced a little when he moved his hips. He was by no means out of shape, but he wasn't very experienced in activities such as these and clearly he was feeling it. Connor seemed to have noticed too because he moved a hand down to rest on Devon's waist. "Does it hurt?"

Devon shook his head, still refusing to look up at Connor. It wasn't a bad pain or even very strong, just annoying to deal with.

"Had you… done this before?"

Devon dug his fingers into Connor's skin at the question. "Don't ask that now! Yes or no, it's embarrassing and I don't want to ruin the moment." Despite his inexperience, he did still have *some* experience. His first time having sex was nothing he was proud of and he was on the path to repeating his past if he wasn't careful.

Connor was quiet for a moment. "I thought —"

"Would you answer that question if I asked?" Devon cut him off before he could finish his thought.

Connor shrugged. "I suppose so. But yeah, it doesn't really matter right now." They were both quiet for a moment after that, until Connor finally asked, "Are you hungry?"

Devon nodded and finally rolled to lay next to Connor. He had been hungry since before he even made a move on Connor. He'd just gotten so caught up in the heat of the moment that he forgot until now. "I could eat."

Connor carefully sat up, making sure he didn't displace Devon too much. "I'll bring the food here."

"I can get up." Devon didn't need to be spoiled with food in bed again. That made it feel too intimate and this was just sex, right? They were still new to dating and Devon wasn't about to rush anymore than he already had.

"But if you're sore…" Connor looked at Devon with his brow furrowed. He rested a hand on Devon's shoulder.

Devon shrugged his hand off and pushed himself up. He got out of bed and, despite his legs feeling sore, he walked to Connor. "See? I'm fine."

Connor still looked at him with a concerned expression on his face, but he slowly nodded. He went to his closet and got out some pajama pants for himself and a clean shirt for Devon. He handed it to him. "Here."

He took the shirt and looked at it for a moment before slipping it over his head. He hadn't thought he was that much smaller than Connor, but when he put the shirt on, it looked a bit oversized. The sight made Connor smile, which only made Devon's face turn red. He stalked past Connor and out the bedroom door. "I don't want to eat cold food."

"It would've been warm if we'd eaten it when I first made it." Connor followed after him and rested his hand on Devon's waist.

Devon glared up at him. "Are you complaining about what happened?"

Connor shook his head. "No, of course not." He leaned over and kissed the side of

Devon's head. "I'll heat up the food, don't worry."

He chuckled. It seemed almost easy to get Connor to do what he wanted, at least small things. He walked with Connor to the kitchen and propped himself up to sit on the counter. Connor went to the stove to turn the heat back on the food he'd made earlier, but froze when he saw Devon. Devon raised a brow and tilted his head. "What?"

What Connor was staring at was Devon's bare ass on the counter and the way his legs were spread just enough. Devon realized where Connor's gaze was and quickly shut his knees. He pulled the shirt down to cover his groin, keeping his hands there. "Food first..." he said as he turned his head.

Connor nodded and took a deep breath. He stared at the food in the pan, his gaze not wavering to look up at Devon even for a moment. Devon did the same, looking all around the kitchen except at Connor's broad shoulders. But as he looked around the kitchen, he could tell that this was the most loved room in the apartment. All of the appliances were new and there were extra kinds of appliances on the counter tops that Devon didn't even know what they were. Everything was neatly organized and there were even a few photographs of food on the walls. No wonder Connor invested in a restaurant, he was a foodie.

Not long after Connor heated up the food, he served the noodles onto two plates. He turned off the stove and added Thai basil garnish to make the dish have a nice presentation. He held a plate out to Devon. "It's all hot now."

Devon stared down at the plate and slowly reached out to take it. He glanced up at Connor. "How come you're not the chef in that restaurant you own?"

"Invest in," Connor corrected. He helped Devon off the counter and guided him to the kitchen table. "I love food, but I don't want to make it my career."

Devon nodded. He could understand that. Enjoying something and making a career out of it were two very different things. Not that he even knew what he enjoyed or wanted to make a career out of… He sat down at the table and poked the food with his fork. "I almost feel bad eating it. It looks too good."

Connor chuckled. "I hope you do eat it and enjoy it or I might be sad."

Devon chuckled and raised his brow. "Sad? I don't think you'll be shattered if I don't like the food."

"Maybe you should try it first." Connor's expression was far more serious than it had been even a few moments ago.

Devon nodded and took a bite. It really was delicious, such a mix of flavors. He licked his lips and nodded. "Well you don't have to be sad, this food is pretty good."

Connor grinned. "I'm glad to hear it." He started to eat too.

CHAPTER 12

Connor was awake early in the morning. To him, this was a normal time to be awake around the time of sunrise. But Devon was still curled up in his bed, fast asleep. He hadn't realized how much of a night person Devon was until now. He couldn't say anything against it since they'd both taken plenty advantage of that last night. He hadn't planned to go quite so far yesterday, but as soon as Devon made that first move, Connor wasn't holding back.

He laid back down and carefully pulled Devon into his arms. Not long ago, Devon had been digging his fingers into Connor's shoulders, trying to hide his face against the side of his arm. But every sight of Devon's pink cheeks as he let out such delicate moans made Connor want to hold him closer. Devon stirred and Connor froze, wondering if Devon would actually wake up. But he didn't seem to wake up, so he gently rested his head with his nose in Devon's hair. That sweet honey smell was still there. That same smell could make him so aroused or, in moments like this, could be such a gentle comfort. He'd never felt this with Zach before. He closed his eyes and took a deep breath.

Connor stayed in bed with Devon for a while. It was a Saturday, so he didn't have to go into the office. Thank goodness because it was already midmorning and Devon was still sleeping soundly. He didn't think he'd gone that hard on Devon, but maybe the omega really had been a virgin?

Regardless, Connor carefully pulled himself away. He'd love to stay in bed all day with Devon if he could, but his stomach was saying otherwise. He got into pajamas again and went to the door. He paused and looked back at Devon, asleep in his bed. Even the way his lips were slightly parted and how he was clutching onto the pillow was cute to Connor. He smiled and quietly walked out.

He went to the kitchen and inwardly cursed himself for not cleaning any of the dishes last night. At the same time, was he really going to choose washing dishes over making love to Devon? Unlikely. Devon's lips had been so soft against his own. Devon's skin had been just as soft and Connor couldn't resist placing feathery kisses all over him, making Devon giggle.

He took the plates to the sink. The sauce had crusted onto the plates, but a little soak in the sink and it would come right off. Connor got food out for breakfast. He still wasn't sure what kind of food Devon loved. He'd eaten the breakfast he'd made him last time, but he'd eaten it so slowly that Connor had to wonder if Devon hadn't liked it. Still, the memory of Devon nibbling on toast was making Connor smile without even realizing it.

Connor decided to make another hearty breakfast. After all of the activity last night, Devon had to be hungry, Connor certainly was. He got several things cooking and put on a pot of tea. The food was almost ready, but he hadn't heard any sign of Devon waking up. As much as he didn't want to wake him, he didn't want Devon to complain about the heat of this meal too. He let out a breath and shook his head. He poured Devon a mug of tea and brought it with him as he walked back to the bedroom.

Devon was still sleeping there, in the same position Connor had left him in. He chuckled to himself and set the mug down and gently sat on the edge of the bed by Devon. He rested a hand on Devon's shoulder. "Morning."

"Mm?" Devon scrunched his face up and brought a hand up to rub his eyes.

Connor chuckled and pushed some of Devon's hair out of his face. "Good morning."

"Already?" Devon mumbled and curled up more into a ball.

"Yeah, it is." He chuckled, seeing a grumpy Devon was actually pretty cute. "Hungry?"

Devon shook his head. "Wanna sleep."

"Well, that'll be too bad, the food might be cold if you go back to sleep." Connor chuckled. "I can bring it to you in bed?"

"No, I'm not weak." Devon glared up at Connor and pulled the covers around him tighter.

"Can't I want to do something nice for my boyfriend?"

"Boyfriend?" Devon stared up at him, eyes wide.

Connor tilted his head to the side, unsure of where this surprise was coming from. "Well, we're dating and we've slept together, so I thought—"

"You thought what?" Devon interrupted before Connor could finish. "Isn't that rather *alpha* of you?" Devon sat up, wincing as he moved. "I'm not property that can be claimed by spreading my legs."

Their eyes were inches from each other and Connor was holding Devon's gaze back steadily, refusing to back down. Devon certainly was a feisty omega, but Connor wasn't wrong and he knew it. "You spread your own legs. I didn't force you."

Devon's cheeks turned pink, but his gaze hardened.

Connor stood up, looking down at Devon. "You can either eat a hot breakfast now or a cold one whenever you feel so inclined to get out of bed." He turned without waiting for a response and walked out of the bedroom. This wasn't how he imagined the morning after would go.

He stalked back to the kitchen and set his own plate on the table. He got himself a glass of orange juice and sat down with a thud. Despite his cold words, he waited a few minutes to eat. But Devon didn't appear, so he started to eat.

Several minutes after he'd started, Devon stumbled into the kitchen, fully dressed. So that's how it was going to go? He said one thing Devon didn't like and he was leaving?

"I thought you made breakfast for both of us." Devon stared at the table and Connor's plate. Connor leaned back and crossed his arms over his chest. The other plate was sitting on the counter, it was obvious to him, surely Devon would see it if he looked. Devon spun on his heel. "Whatever."

Connor let him get to the doorway before he said, "It's on the counter."

Devon stopped and looked back at the counter. He took a step towards it, slowly picking up the warm plate. He turned to the table, avoiding eye contact with Connor as he took a seat.

"Maybe we can relax more today." Connor reached a hand towards Devon, but Devon shoved his hands in his jacket pocket. "We could watch a show, talk about—"

"I should go." Devon stood up.

"Aren't you going to eat?" Connor's chest felt so tight.

Devon took a step towards the doorway, his back to Connor. "I'm not hungry anyways."

Connor shook his head. "Is this really how you're going to be?"

"Me?!" Devon spun around to look at Connor again. "You're the one pushing things so fast!"

"How?" Connor stood up. "You were pretty happy with this pace last night. I let you sleep in, I made breakfast for you to be ready when you woke up and I was kind with you. "

"You're not now." Devon shoved his hands in his pockets.

"Well maybe because you got super sensitive when I mentioned being serious with you. You're the one fully dressed and about to walk out on me. Don't dare spin this the other way." Connor was not about to put up with this level of bullshit.

"I don't want to…" Devon mumbled and looked away, shoving his hands deeper into his pockets.

Connor let out a breath and walked up to him. He rested his hands on Devon's arms. "Then don't leave. Stay and have something to eat with me."

Devon melted into Connor's arms, leaning against him and hiding his face against his shoulder. He gripped tightly onto Connor's shirt. Connor wrapped his arms around him and rubbed his back. He leaned his cheek against Devon's head. He could get used to this.

But Devon's shoulders started trembling. He pushed himself back after a minute, shaking his head. "It's better if we aren't serious." He walked to the plate of food and grabbed a piece and ate it. "Mm, fuck…"

"What do you mean, Devon?" Connor walked up to him and touched his arm again.

Devon flinched and walked out of the kitchen without looking at Connor. Connor followed him in time to see him pat his pockets down and pull his phone out. "That late already? I gotta go." But Connor could see that the phone screen didn't even turn on. Devon bolted to the door and pulled it open. "I'll call you." He dashed out without even looking back at Connor once.

Connor stared at the shut door, eyes wide and mouth agape. He didn't want to believe any of that had happened. Maybe he was still sleeping and he would wake up next to Devon after all. He waited at the door for a minute, hoping Devon would walk back through it, but no one came.

"You're my best friend. I'll call you." The sound of Zach's voice rang in his head with the echo of the door slamming. The last time he'd seen Zach was when he'd been dashing out before breakfast. It took Zach a year to leave. It only took Devon two dates.

"Fuck!" Connor yelled and turned around, grabbing a pillow off the couch and heaving it across the room. He should never have let his guard down, it was way too soon to get attached and now the only person he wanted just walked out of his life. He didn't believe for a second that Devon would call. Even if he did, maybe Connor wouldn't answer.

CHAPTER 13

Devon slumped down in the elevator as he rode it down. He covered his face with his palms. What had he been thinking? He should never have even done it with Connor in the first place. He didn't really regret the feeling. Connor knew how to make him feel good, but he'd rushed things and now he just wanted to slow down.

His eyes stung. He looked up at the lights on the ceiling of the elevator, trying to dry his eyes. He was still damn hungry and getting that piece from what Connor had made only made him hungrier. Why did he have to walk out on a warm, home-cooked meal? His whole body was aching as if he could feel every single one of his regrets.

When the elevator doors opened, he scrambled back to his feet and stumbled out of the elevator. He wasn't tired, he'd slept enough, but still walking all the way home seemed too difficult. He stepped outside of the apartment building and looked around. He didn't know downtown well despite living in Mount Oolie his whole life. He pulled his phone out and checked his transit app. He walked to the nearest bus stop and waited.

Mount Oolie wasn't huge, but it wasn't small either and it had a decent public transit system. Many people used the buses, but then there were also people like Devon who preferred to walk where they wanted to go.

Devon sank down onto the bench as he waited for the bus. He must've just missed one because he sat there for 15 minutes before the bus finally arrived. He got on and made his way to the back. He wanted the long bench to stretch out. The bus was quiet for a Saturday, but Devon figured it was because it was still morning.

Devon closed his eyes, leaning against the back of the seat. The rhythmic jostling of the bus was lulling him to sleep. And sleep he did. Until the bus came to a screeching halt. Devon sat up and rubbed his eyes, disoriented for a moment. He looked outside and realized he'd missed his stop. "Shit."

He sat up straight and pulled the cord to request the next stop. He was close enough to home now that he could walk the few extra blocks home. The bus started moving again and pulled up to the next stop. Devon hopped off as soon as the doors were open and took off walking at a brisk pace home.

Halfway down the block, he had to stop. His legs were not agreeing with him. He stood there for a moment, taking a deep breath before forcing a foot forward, this time at a more moderate pace.

On the steps leading up to his front door, a small, black and white tuxedo cat with a pink nose sat there, staring at him. As he got close, she let out such a sad meow as if she were crying. He reached down to pet her, but she quickly dashed away.

Several minutes later, he was fumbling through his pockets, looking for his house key. He checked his jacket and his pants, but he didn't seem to have his keys. Had he forgotten them at Connor's? Oh that would be awkward... he wanted to see Connor again, but maybe not for another week at least.

Before he could do anything about his keys, the front door opened in front of him. He gulped. "Hey Mom."

She smiled, though her eyes didn't match her lips. She stepped back to let him in. "How was your date last night?"

He walked in, his head hung and his hands still shoved in his pockets. He didn't make eye contact with her, he couldn't bring himself to look at her. "It was fine." He kicked his shoes off inside the door and took his hoodie off. He shrugged. "Probably won't see him again. I'm sure you'll be happy about that."

She touched his arm. "Why would I be happy about that?"

"Just…" He looked away. "I know you think I'm not ready for things like that."

"And you think it would make me happy to know you won't see him again?" She let out a long sigh. "Devon… that's not what I want. I don't want you to be unhappy. I just don't want you to get hurt."

He shrugged and took a few steps towards the stairs. "I do a good job of hurting people myself, if I get hurt, it's just payback."

"Devon." She jogged a few steps to catch up to him. "You're a good person, you're not hurting people."

He finally looked back at her. "Aren't I hurting you? Saying I'd be home soon, but staying out until the next morning?"

"I didn't panic this time because I knew you'd be out." She smiled, concern creasing her brow. "You're not a bad person, Devon."

He nodded slowly and looked back upstairs. "I think I might just go back to bed."

"Are you hungry?" She rubbed his arm. "I can make some pancakes. With chocolate, just how you like."

He chuckled a bit and nodded. "I am hungry, I wouldn't say no to your pancakes."

She smiled and brought him to the kitchen. "That's better."

• • •

Devon was leaning against the counter at Almond Blossom Tea, staring at his phone, specifically his messages with Connor. He'd texted him to say he'd probably forgotten his keys there, but he hadn't heard back yet. He checked the timestamps, it hadn't been too long, but Connor had always been prompt at responding before.

Someone shoved him in the side pushing him away from the counter. He looked up to see Robbie and rolled his eyes. Would that snappy blonde ever give him a break? Robbie set down two drinks on the pickup counter where Devon had just been and called out the order.

"Still doing my job for me, I see." Devon shoved his phone back in his pocket.

"Still daydreaming about Prince Charming, I see." Robbie glared back at him. "Do you have to rub it in?"

"I didn't say shit about him." Devon crossed his arms. Robbie was the last person he wanted to talk to about Connor. Robbie would laugh him out of the cafe if he knew what happened.

"I can see it in your face. Your moony eyes and staring at your phone all the time. We do have customers to attend to, you know?"

Robbie stalked past Devon towards the register even though there was no one in line.

"Yeah, well, you seem to have that covered."

Robbie whipped around. "I'm sick of doing your job for you!"

Devon stood up straight and looked down at Robbie. "Well, maybe if you told me what orders you needed, you wouldn't be doing my damn job! You want me to work with you, but you micromanage the shit out of me even though you're my peer, not my boss."

"I don't!" Robbie jutted out his lower lip. "You just need to be more attentive!"

"You mean like when there are no orders to make?" Devon sneered.

"There were!"

"And you didn't say shit to me about it!"

"Get your head out of your phone then!"

"I'm fully present right now, aren't I?"

It was only when someone cleared their throat that either of them looked over. Devon gulped when he saw Kieran staring at both of them. The few customers that were in the cafe were watching and whispering to each other.

Robbie and Devon both looked at each other and then pointed at each other and in unison, said, "He started it."

Kieran let out a long sigh and rubbed his temples. "Step in the back room."

They both nodded and walked into the back. Robbie glared at Devon. "If I get fired, it is so your fault."

"My fault?" Devon stopped and glared at him. "You're the one picking on me."

"You're the one slacking off."

Before Devon could respond, Kieran walked in and closed the door behind him. "I don't want to get involved in whatever's going on between you two, but when it's affecting my business, I have to." They were both silent, so Kieran explained, "Arguing like that in front of the customers? Not acceptable. I let you both get away with a lot, but you've gone too far."

"This wouldn't have happened if Devon would just do his job," Robbie mumbled and looked away.

Devon glared at him. He opened his mouth to speak, but Kieran spoke first. "One of you is going home today because I cannot have you arguing like that again. I'll let you choose who goes home, but both of your schedules will be changing. I won't have you two working together anymore."

"Fine. I'll go home today." Devon went and grabbed his coat.

"Real shocker." Robbie rolled his eyes.

Devon gripped onto his coat tighter. Oh how he wanted to spit something back at Robbie, but clearly now was not the time. He pulled his coat on and walked past Robbie, looking at Kieran. "Just tell me when you want me to come in again."

He walked out of the room without waiting for a response and promptly left the cafe without another word.

CHAPTER 14

"Why do you think that my kitchen is for your moping?" Tristan snapped when he walked out of the freezer and saw Connor leaning against the counter.

Connor shrugged and kept eating the carrot one of the sous chefs had given him. "Your employees don't seem to mind."

Tristan rolled his eyes. "They don't mind because they know you put your money into this place. They probably think they'll lose their salaries if they kick you out. Me, on the other hand, I think I'll lose my customers if I let you stay."

"Well, that's a nice way to treat your friend when I came here to talk to you." Connor took another bite and snapped the carrot with his teeth.

"Who did you break up with this time?" Tristan let out a breath.

"You know what, maybe I will come back later." Connor stood up straight and picked up another carrot before walking towards the back door.

"Do you have to pout like that?" Tristan called after him.

"Aren't I doing what you want?" Connor stopped and looked over his shoulder.

Tristan let out a long breath and his shoulders sagged. "No. Let's just take this conversation to the office before anything burns."

Connor nodded and followed Tristan to the back office. Tristan usually made do with Connor lurking in the kitchen, he figured he must look really bad if Tristan was suggesting they continue their conversation somewhere else. Connor walked into the office and sat down without even saying a word.

Tristan closed the door behind him and sat down, too. He looked directly at Connor, leaning forward in his chair. "Okay, what's wrong?"

"Maybe nothing's wrong."

"Bullshit. You don't come in here like everything's on fire when it's something small." Tristan leaned back and crossed his arms and stared at Connor.

"He doesn't want to date. He wants to be casual."

"Maybe there wasn't chemistry?" Tristan shrugged.

Connor shook his head. "No, he made the first move."

"You're kidding." Tristan leaned in. "He made the first move and also dumped you on the same date? What kind of omega is he?"

"Do you have to be such an ass about it?" Connor glared back at him.

"It's pretty surprising, you gotta admit." Tristan leaned back, eyes still wide. "Most omegas are like 'mark me!' after the first time doing it. You did follow through, right?"

"I did not leave him unsatisfied."

"Like he left you?"

"Fuck you." Connor rolled his eyes.

"Oh, come on, you know what I'm like. If you wanted comfort, you would've talked to somebody else." Tristan shrugged and Connor shook his head and let out a short laugh. Tristan continued, "Who knows, maybe you'll find somebody else, someone who smells even better than he did."

"Yeah." Connor nodded. "It's frustrating to go after someone and get turned down like that. For only two dates, I did a lot for him." He was trying to act like he didn't care about Devon, but in all honesty, he could care less about having to put in effort. Connor thought that he and Devon could have something special. He wished Devon had felt the same way.

● ● ●

Connor was sitting alone in his office again, watching everyone come back from their lunch break. He kept twiddling the pen between his fingers. Everyone seemed so happy, he wondered how many of them were already happily mated. Connor clutched the pen in his fist.

There was a knock on his door and he looked up to see Riley. He suddenly let go of the pen that he'd almost broken in his hand. He stood up and went to the door, opening it and beckoning her in. "Hey, I thought you were still out to lunch."

"Just got back." She smiled and walked in, taking a seat across from his desk.

He sat down too and looked at her. "Is there something I can do?"

"Are you…" she paused and looked down. "Still okay with the finance team doing a team lunch tomorrow?"

He furrowed his brow. "Yeah, we settled that already, you have a budget for it." He leaned forward. "Is that really what you came to ask?"

"It isn't." She took another breath and looked up at Connor. "You look like you did when Zach left and, well, I'm concerned you're going to fall back into that rut."

He nodded slowly and leaned back. "Thanks for the honesty."

"I didn't mean to insult you." She rubbed her temple. "You can't build a relationship with Devon if you're still pining over Zach."

"I won't be building a relationship with him."

"What?" Riley furrowed her brow and leaned closer.

"He doesn't want anything serious." It hurt every time he said it aloud. He didn't want it to be over between him and Devon so quickly.

"I'm sorry to hear that." She tentatively reached out and rested a hand on his arm. Connor relaxed and didn't pull away. She smiled. "I'm sure you'll be able to meet someone else soon."

"That's it!" Connor sat up straight with a wide grin. "I'll make him jealous by pursuing someone else."

"That isn't what I said at all…" Riley stared at him, eyes wide, like he'd suddenly grown a second head.

"I know, but I don't want someone else, I want him and I'm not done trying to get him." He grinned and pulled out his phone. "If you'll excuse me, I have a phone call to make."

She blinked a few times before slowly standing up and nodding. "Well, if you need me, you know where to find me." She turned and walked out of his office.

Connor scrolled back through the calls on his phone, looking for the one from that other barista. He'd seen the way those two bickered, if he did anything with that blonde barista, surely Devon would be jealous.

He finally found the number and called. It only took a couple rings before someone answered. "Hello?" Connor did recognize the voice of the other barista, but for the life of him, could not remember his name.

"Hi, this is Connor Thorton, we spoke the other day." Connor said, hoping the barista would introduce himself.

"Oh, hello~!" The barista's tone instantly changed and softened. "I hope you're doing well!"

"I am." Connor said with a smile, "I'm wondering if you'll be free tomorrow night?"

"Really?! Sure!" The excitement in his voice was unmistakable. "I mean... I'm probably available, what did you have in mind?"

Connor was starting to feel bad for even calling the barista. He didn't mean to get his hopes up and dash them... but if it didn't work to make Devon jealous, he could at least give this omega a chance. "I was thinking we could go to dinner. I can meet you at the cafe."

"Oh, that would be perfect," the barista said. Connor could practically hear him smiling. "What time?"

"I'll come by around closing. Does that work?"

"That'll be great! See you soon, Connor." The barista giggled.

"See you soon." Connor chuckled and quickly hung up. He just made a date with someone whose name he didn't even know... He smacked his palm to his forehead and let out an exasperated sigh.

CHAPTER 15

Devon leaned up against the counter, glaring daggers at the back of Robbie's head. They'd had their own shifts, each of them working with Kieran at different times of the day and days of the week, but today was the first shift he'd had with Robbie since they argued in front of the customers. Kieran warned them that if it happened again, they'd both be fired, so Devon had been keeping his mouth shut the entire day.

But Robbie, on the other hand, was happily strutting about and getting chatty with the customers. He seemed to leave the drink making to Devon, so Devon actually did some work today, but something felt fishy.

When there was a lull between orders, he checked his phone. He hadn't gotten any response from Connor about his house keys and his mom kept putting him off about getting another set made. She said she would, but each day she came back claiming to have been too busy or just forgotten. It felt like she was trying to make him get his keys back from Connor. He would if he could.

When the last customer finally walked out and the cafe was empty, Devon finally spoke, "What are you doing here?"

"Working," was all Robbie said before making himself a boba.

Devon narrowed his eyes and didn't take his eyes off the blonde. "You weren't supposed to work today."

"Kieran's been working all day every day because you couldn't keep your mouth shut and do your work the other day." Robbie put a straw through the lid of his cup. "I'm just being nice and working a day with you so he can get a break from you."

Devon rolled his eyes. "Bullshit. There's no way he would've agreed to that."

"Well, I asked him and he said yes." Robbie set his drink down and put his hands on his hips. "So deal with it."

"I'm not the one with a problem. You were the one getting mad at me for nothing." He glared back.

Robbie was about to respond when the door to the cafe opened. He looked at the door and back at Devon. "I'd love to continue this conversation, but I have to do my job."

Devon bit his lip so hard, he almost drew blood. He really wished he could just bite Robbie's head off. On the bright side, they were busy enough for the rest of the shift that there wasn't a time when they were alone. Devon avoided talking to Robbie for the rest of the shift.

It was almost time to close and the cafe had emptied out again. Devon was about to get his coat and head out early to leave the cleanup to Robbie, but the door opened and Devon looked up. He was shocked to see Connor walking up to the front counter. Before Robbie could even get to the register, Devon swooped in and took the spot.

"I thought you weren't ever going to come back." Did he sound desperate or angry? Honestly, he couldn't tell. He said that he wanted to take things slow and Connor started ignoring him? Not cool.

"I'm doing what you wanted." Connor's voice was cold and he gave Devon a hard stare.

"Well, what do you want to drink? You can't just loiter here," Devon mumbled bitterly.

"I'll have a strawberry milk tea with boba, and I'm not loitering." Connor furrowed his brow.

Devon noticed how he still ordered his favorite. Damn, why did he have to be so conflicted every time he saw this handsome alpha? "Then give me back my keys next time you come by."

"So you want me to bring them?"

"What else would you do?" Devon shrugged.

"You don't want to come pick them up yourself?" Connor spoke more softly.

Devon's gut twisted and he felt so bad for walking out on him last weekend. "Didn't think you would want me to…"

Connor paid for his drink and shoved his wallet back into his pocket. "We'll see."

He walked away to wait at a table and pulled his phone out.

Devon couldn't stop staring. Suddenly, Robbie's voice sounded right beside his ear. "Don't you dare get any ideas. He has plans with *me* today."

"What?!" Devon could not stop himself from yelling. He whipped around to face Robbie. There's no way it could be true. "You're lying."

Robbie smirked. "Nuhuh. Just watch." He flung his apron to the side and swished his hips as he walked over to Connor's table. It was like he was putting on a show for Devon more than Connor. He smiled at Connor and touched his shoulder. "I'll be ready in just a few minutes, Connor~"

Connor nodded, smiling up at Robbie. "Sounds good, Sweetie."

Devon's jaw dropped.

There was no way this could actually be happening. And Connor calling Robbie 'sweetie'? Just how long had this been going on? Clearly there was a lot going on behind his back, how else would they have gotten so close to be using such pet names.

Robbie turned and grinned at Devon as he sauntered back over to the counter. "Who's a liar now?"

"Clearly, still you since you've been seeing him behind my back." Devon snapped. He yanked his own apron off and tossed it aside. "Do whatever you want, Robbie, see if I care." He stormed into the back room, snatching his jacket off the hook.

Robbie tried to stop him when he came back out. "Hey! You can't leave, the cafe needs to be cleaned and shut down for the night."

"You do it." Devon purposely smacked his shoulder against Robbie's as he stalked out of the cafe. He could feel Robbie's eyes lingering on him, but he didn't look back to see.

His eyes stung and he wiped them dry with the back of his hand. He had asked for nothing serious and that's just what he'd gotten... nothing. He didn't even pay attention to where he was going, his feet just kept moving. His insides kept twisting, replaying the scene in his mind over and over. He'd made it too easy for Connor and now he was over him.

That was it, wasn't it? Fucking alphas. Take what they want from you and give nothing back... He wanted to wash away these ugly feelings in his heart. He shouldn't feel jealous over someone he hardly knew, but why wasn't he good enough?!

Devon couldn't take another step, his feet just wouldn't move. Everything was so empty. He crouched down on the ground, sitting back on his feet. He didn't care that he was in the middle of the sidewalk, it wasn't busy this time of night anyways. He hung his head in his hands, his palms becoming unbearably wet. He could just kick himself for letting himself get attached after two dates.

"Hey cutie! Need a ride?" The unmistakable scent of an alpha reached his nose. Except this smell was not pleasant and made him want to hurl or punch something, he couldn't decide which. He lifted his head up. A car had pulled up next to him, the window rolled down. The alpha didn't even bother getting out of the car.

"Fuck you."

"Yeah, what's your price?" The alpha smirked. "I love a crier."

Devon stood up and flipped the guy off. He took a quick look around, realizing he'd walked right into the heart of the Meadows—arguably the worst neighborhood in town. No wonder he'd been propositioned like that. There weren't brothels in this neighborhood anymore, but the same energy lingered. Not far from where he was standing, there was the most well-known strip club in Mount Oolie— Omega Lounge. This was certainly not the kind of place he should've ever stopped in.

He started to walk down the street again, hoping he could find his way to a better street. The car next to him kept driving slowly alongside him. "Come on, cutie. How much for an hour?"

"A fuck like you could even last that long?" Devon couldn't hold his tongue.

"Make it two, but the second one's on you," the alpha's voice deepened, almost getting to that demanding point.

"I'm not a goddamn whore!" He walked faster, but the car would not drive away.

"Listen here, prude—!"

"He said no." A familiar voice came from behind Devon.

He whipped around to see Kieran glaring over his shoulder at the driver. "What are you —?"

"Oh, there's two of you? I'll take a threesome." The alpha smirked.

"I don't share." Kieran grabbed Devon by the shoulders and started to drag him down the block.

"H-Hey!" Devon stumbled the first few steps before rushing to keep up with Kieran.

The alpha drove a little faster to try and keep up with them, but Kieran quickly ducked them into an apartment building doorway and out of sight. It was an old building with a metal gate blocking the way up the apartments, but there was enough of an alcove that Kieran and Devon could hide in. Devon squirmed in Kieran's grip. "Let go of me!"

"Shut up! What if he's still out there?" Kieran hissed. He leaned forward, peeking around the corner of the doorway. The car was still there, engine idling.

"What are you even doing here?" Devon snapped quietly.

"Saving your ass. Happy?" Kieran let out a long breath and leaned back against the cement wall, rubbing his temple.

"I mean, I guess? But seriously, how did you know I was here? I didn't even know I was here!" Devon accidentally started to raise his voice.

Kieran covered Devon's mouth with his palm. "Seriously, can we wait until that guy is gone?" Devon smacked his hand away, but stayed quiet. Kieran glanced outside again and the street was indeed empty now. He poked his head out a little further and looked up and down the block. "Okay, let's go."

"Go where?"

"My apartment." Kieran stepped outside and Devon followed right after. "You can stay or get a ride from there or something."

"I can walk home." Devon shoved his hands in his pockets.

"And have that happen again? I don't want to follow you around all night, you know." Kieran started walking down the street and turned at the corner.

"Where is your apartment anyways? We're still walking in this neighborhood." Devon noticed that they were heading a block deeper into the Meadows.

"I live here." Kieran said plainly.

"In the Meadows?" Devon stared at him as they walked and finally stopped a few blocks away.

Kieran nodded and opened up the old building's metal gate. It was a rundown, old building, but not so old that it had character. It looked like it was built in the 70s and hadn't been kept up since. Faded wallpaper was peeling off the walls in the hall as they walked up the wooden steps up to the third floor.

"Seriously, you live here?" Devon couldn't stop looking around. It seemed like the entire building was covered in a layer of dust.

"Yeah, why?" Kieran looked back at Devon as he unlocked his door.

"I dunno, it just doesn't seem like… you." Devon scratched his head.

Kieran sighed and opened the door. "Just how much money do you think my cafe makes?"

"Like, a decent amount," Devon answered nonchalantly as he walked inside. There was a small pile of shoes by the door, so Devon took his own shoes off.

Kieran walked in and did the same, closing the door behind him. "If it did, do you think I would only have two employees?"

"I kind of just assumed that I never had shifts with other employees…" Devon looked away and scratched the back of his neck.

"It's just you and Robbie." Kieran walked into his apartment. It was a studio, so everything was all together in the one room. Even as little space as there was, Kieran kept it nice and tidy, so it didn't feel too small. But Devon did notice how the whole place was about the size of his bedroom in his mom's house.

Devon didn't move from the spot by the door. "Maybe I should just get that ride home…"

"Do you need to call your mom or are you going to get a Lyft?" Kieran sat down on his bed, looking at Devon.

Devon shrugged. "Lyft, I guess. It's probably late to call my mom."

Kieran furrowed his brow, looking at him. "You can come in more. My apartment is small, but it's not that bad."

Devon took a step inside. "I guess it's just weird that the whole place feels like a bedroom."

Kieran laughed. "Afraid to sit on a bed with me? Don't worry, I'm not going to do anything to you."

Devon did relax a little. He didn't really think Kieran would do something, but it still felt awkward to him. Kieran stretched out on his bed and pointed across the room. "You can use one of my table chairs if it would make you more comfortable."

Devon did indeed go to the small, two-seater table and sat in one of the chairs.

Kieran turned only his head to look at him. "Better?" Devon nodded. "Can I ask you something?"

"Yeah, sure." Devon shrugged.

"Why were you in the Meadows in the first place?" Kieran propped himself up on his elbows.

"I don't know... I just kept walking." Devon looked away, shrinking back against the chair. "Took a wrong turn."

"Tree Streets is in the opposite direction of the Meadows." Kieran stared at him blankly, waiting for Devon to say more.

"I ran out of the cafe, okay?! Is that what you really want to know?! Why I ditched Robbie at work and almost got picked up like a whore at the docks?!" Devon couldn't stop himself from yelling. His hands gripped tightly onto his pants, crushing the fabric. Devon turned his head, unable to look back at Kieran. His eyes were stinging again and he was beginning to hate the sensation.

"It's something with that guy you're seeing, isn't it?" Kieran's voice was quiet yet firm. He sat up and moved to the side of his bed so he could look at Devon directly. He reached a hand towards Devon, but let his hand fall short and rested it on his own leg.

"I'm so not seeing him anymore." Devon crossed his arms over his chest.

"Why not?" Kieran scooted a little closer, his brow furrowed.

"He's been seeing Robbie behind my back, I'm no one's whore!"

"Really? That's weird that Robbie didn't say anything about it if he was seeing someone. Robbie's not the best at keeping secrets…" Kieran rubbed his chin, sitting up a little straighter.

"What does it matter?" Devon threw his hands in the air. "Maybe I should just be someone's bitch!"

"Devon. You're no one's bitch. Why would you think that about yourself?" Kieran leaned forward. His stern gaze was fixed right on Devon, making Devon shift in his seat.

"Because it's true. I had something promising, or so I thought, with Connor and I just went headfirst into sex with him because it's all alphas want and it's all I know how to even do. It's not like I'm an interesting person. I'm boring as fuck." Everything spilled out of Devon, once he started, he couldn't stop. He'd never intended to talk to Kieran about any of it.

Kieran's brow creased and he leaned closer. His tone was very serious as he asked, "Did he force you to do things?"

Devon shook his head. "No... I basically offered myself up because I assumed he wanted it. And he must have since he took me up on that offer."

"Are you sure that is what he wanted?"

"What do you mean? I didn't force him to fuck me!"

Kieran let out a sigh. "He might have wanted you for more than sex, but you seem... used... to only being wanted for sex, so that's all you got."

"So it's my fault now? My fault that he's calling Robbie 'sweetie'?"

"I didn't say that." Kieran sat up straight. "I meant that if you really care, it might be worth talking to him again." Kieran stood up and went to a closet on the other side of the room. He got out a blanket and a mattress pad. "Here, why don't you stay the night and I'll help you talk to him in the morning?"

"And if I don't want to talk to him?"

"Then I'll tell your mom that you got mixed up with a guy in the Meadows and she'll end up picking you up from work and dropping you off every day."

"You wouldn't!" Devon gulped, eyes wide.

"Try me." Kieran handed Devon the blanket. Devon slowly reached out and took it.

CHAPTER 16

Connor watched the display between Robbie and Devon unfold. He hadn't meant to cause a scene or to hurt Devon this much... If Devon hadn't stopped them from dating in the first place, this would never have happened! But he couldn't blame Devon, even if he wanted to. He could only stare after Devon as he walked out.

It took Connor a moment to realize that Robbie had walked up to him. The blonde barista was in the middle of saying something by the time Connor heard him. He'd missed the whole first half of what he said, but Robbie looked up at him with a sorry smile, "Will that be okay?"

Connor blinked a few times and nodded. "Yes, that'll be fine." He wasn't sure what he'd agreed to, but since Robbie went back behind the counter and started doing some cleaning, he assumed that Robbie would have a little extra work to do. Connor sat back down at his table and brought his palm to his face. What had he just done?

He watched Robbie work before pulling his phone out again. He was glad that Robbie was so preoccupied, it gave him time to scroll through his messages with Devon. Connor typed out a long message, asking Devon to come back and tried to explain himself, but he just couldn't hit send.

"Sorry about that, I'm all ready to go."

The sudden sound of Robbie's voice above him, made Connor look up. He quickly locked his phone and shoved it back in his pocket. He smiled and stood up. "Alright, I'm ready, too."

He walked out of the cafe with Robbie and started walking to Rose Gold. He didn't mean to recreate the same date he had with Devon, but he wanted Tristan to be able to get a glimpse of Robbie. After the scene with Devon, Connor would certainly be talking to Tristan about it.

Robbie followed alongside him and glommed onto his arm. Connor swallowed and kept looking forward. Robbie's scent reached his nose and it took Connor quite some effort to keep from making a face like he'd just eaten a lemon. Did Robbie not feel the same about his smell? If he did, Connor couldn't tell.

"Hopefully, the rest of your day was alright?" Connor tried to make small talk with Robbie.

"Oh, it was so long! I just couldn't wait for it to be done so I could see you~" Robbie looked up at him with a grin.

Was that a sincere smile or was he trying to impress Connor? Connor got the feeling that Robbie was trying to appear more interested than he was. Devon had never forced himself to be interested, he *was* interested. Connor sighed to himself and smiled back at Robbie. "I'm glad we're here now, Robbie."

"Oh, but I liked it when you called me sweetie!" Robbie's lower lip jutted out. On someone else, Connor might've found such a pouty expression cute, but he was becoming more and more frustrated with this date and didn't find anything desirable about it.

"Don't worry, it's still early in the evening." He wanted to put off using that term of endearment again. He wished he could've saved it for Devon. He should've asked for Robbie's name when he first set up the date...

"What is the plan for this evening?" Robbie kept looking up at Connor as they walked.

Luckily, they were walking up to Rose Gold and Connor could finally get his arm back. He opened the door for Robbie. "I made a reservation for dinner here."

"Oh, I've always wanted to try this place!" Robbie grinned and walked inside.

Connor started to wonder if enough people actually came to their restaurant... He followed Robbie inside and nodded at the host. They smiled as soon as they saw him. They stared at Robbie for a moment, eyes wide. Quickly glancing back at Connor before getting menus for them. They showed Connor and Robbie to the same table he'd sat at with Devon. Connor's insides twisted up at another reminder of Devon and he really regretted bringing Robbie here.

They sat down and Robbie immediately started talking about every item on the menu and what he liked and didn't like about them. Connor furrowed his brow. "I thought you hadn't been here before?"

"Oh, I haven't, I just love good food and some dishes aren't good, no matter how they're cooked!" Robbie giggled and the sound made Connor cringe.

Connor raised his brow and blinked at Robbie a few times. He knew it was Tristan who was cooking, but he still felt a bit insulted. He decided to not mention that he was the main investor. "Then order what you know you like."

"There's so many things that I do like!" Robbie practically squealed and looked over the menu again.

"I'm going to go wash up. I'll be back in a moment." He smiled and stood up.

Robbie smiled. "Hurry back~"

Connor nodded and quickly turned and walked towards the bathrooms. When he was sure Robbie wasn't looking, he ducked into the kitchen instead.

Tristan looked up from where he stood at the stove. "What a surprise…" He got a sous chef to take over. He wiped his hands and walked up to Connor. "What's wrong now?"

Connor rolled his eyes. "I should never have brought Robbie here."

"Who?"

"Robbie, the other barista." Connor rubbed his forehead. "I think this date worked too well to make Devon jealous."

Tristan bit his lip and looked at Connor for a moment before finally speaking, "So what happened? You're here with Robbie, so I take it Devon didn't fall for it?"

Connor shook his head. "No, Devon definitely did, but then he ran out. Now I feel like an asshole towards both of them."

"You are being an asshole to both of them." Tristan crossed his arms.

"Really?" Connor rolled his eyes.

Tristan shrugged, "I'm just spelling it out for you. If you think you can still get Devon back, then he's the one you should be here with, not Robbie."

"And what am I supposed to tell Robbie who's waiting at the table, looking forward to a date?"

"Not every first date is going to be successful." Tristan shrugged and let his hands fall to the side. "You can either make Robbie happy and make yourself miserable, or you can make yourself happy and let Robbie get on with his life."

Connor leaned against the counter and nodded slowly. "I'll talk to him. I may still get him dinner here, but I'll handle it."

Tristan nodded. "Good, you got this. Now I need to get back to my dishes."

Connor opened his mouth to say something else, but turned to leave instead. Tristan was right. It wouldn't be right to lead Robbie on. Connor slowly walked back to the table. A waiter had already brought out water glasses, but hadn't taken the menus. Robbie smiled and waved when he saw him. Connor sat back down. "Sorry for taking so long."

"Is everything okay?" Robbie leaned forward.

A more perfect opportunity could not have offered itself up. Connor took a long breath and shook his head. "I don't think I'm ready to be dating right now."

"What?" Robbie furrowed his brow, tilting his head to the side, not understanding. "You don't want to be here? Am I not as good as Devon? What's so wrong with me? You seemed happy earlier. You called me sweetie!"

Robbie kept going on and Connor felt worse and worse inside. "Robbie, I'm sorry—"

"Sorry?! That just doesn't cut it! Why am I not good enough for you?!" Robbie's voice started to become more shrill as he kept talking.

That sound pierced Connor's ears and something clicked in him. His expression fell flat and he stood up with his shoulders back. "Robbie." His voice was low and commanding. Robbie immediately stopped his rambling. "A waiter will come by and order you a ride home."

Without waiting, Connor turned his back and walked to the kitchen. He felt the eyes of a few diners on him as he walked past. Had they really caused such a scene? Robbie didn't seem to be able to control his volume by the end there. A scene in his own restaurant? His nose curled with disgust.

Connor strolled into the kitchen as if nothing happened. Several employees quickly rushed back to their workstations. Connor furrowed his brow, looking at the employees who kept sneaking glances at him. Whenever one of them made eye contact with him, they immediately looked away and seemed overly focused on the food they were preparing.

Tristan laughed as he walked up. "I wasn't sure you had it in you." He slapped Connor's shoulder.

Connor brought his palm to his face. "Everyone saw what happened, didn't they?"

"Yeah, I saw you tell off that bitchy little omega." Tristan smirked. "Honestly, I didn't think you would."

"What does that mean?" Connor threw his hands up.

Tristan shrugged and glanced to the side. It looked like he was trying hard not to laugh. "I don't know, Ruby. You just... seem a bit soft for an alpha." He looked back at Connor, struggling to hide his smile.

Connor huffed and let out a short laugh. He shook his head. "I choose to practice self control. As a business owner, I have to! It's not like in a restaurant. Rosie."

"Oh? You think I don't know self control?" Tristan crossed his arms, but his expression was still amused. "If I didn't, do you think we'd have this many employees still here?"

"Honestly, I thought you would be like Gordon Ramsey in the kitchen." Connor laughed.

Tristan tried to keep a straight face, but ended up laughing. "Okay, okay, you got me there." He patted Connor's shoulder. "Enough talking to me, go find your omega and mark him before he gets snatched up."

"You just don't know how to take things slow, do you?" Connor laughed.

"Being slow in a kitchen gets the food burned." Tristan smirked.

CHAPTER 17

Devon woke up the next morning, his neck sore as hell. He ended up sleeping on Kieran's mattress pad, but it might as well have been sleeping on the floor. He didn't even feel rested, why was he even awake? He let out a groan and rubbed his eyes. That's when he saw Kieran from the corner of his eyes. He was in the kitchen, preparing something.

"Awake yet?" Kieran walked over to the mattress and looked down at Devon.

"No." Devon rolled over and hid his face on the pillow again.

"I need you to wake up, Devon." Kieran let out a sigh and walked back to the kitchen area. "We need to go back to the cafe."

"We? Don't you mean you?" Devon clung onto the pillow.

"No, I mean you and me." Kieran walked over to him and Devon smelled something tasty. He peeked up and saw that Kieran was holding two plates. "You're supposed to work today, too."

"Too? You really need more employees..." Devon grumbled, slowly sitting up.

"Yeah, I'd like some employees that I didn't have to babysit, but here we are." Kieran sat at the table, setting down the plates.

"I'm not a baby!" But Devon still refused to get up from the mattress.

"Then eat breakfast and go to work like a responsible adult."

Devon wanted to refuse again, but it was pointless. Even if he didn't go to work, he wouldn't be able to stay in Kieran's place. He slowly pushed off the blanket, each movement took all his effort. He crawled his way up to sit at the table. "And if I don't want to be responsible?"

"Then I'm sure your mom would love to know that you were in the Meadows," Kieran said without even looking at Devon.

"You can't use that against me forever." Devon picked up a fork and angrily took a bite.

"It hasn't even been a day. Besides, I don't want to use it against you, I just don't want to fire you." Kieran finished what was left on his plate.

Devon gritted his teeth. Maybe he was making things harder for Kieran and his mom. He didn't know what to do anymore after his attempt at college went so badly. Apparently, he wasn't even cut out to be a barista. He didn't say anything else as he finished eating. He was still dressed, so he was good to go whenever Kieran was. It didn't take them long to head out. Since Kieran wasn't far from the cafe, they walked together. Only when they got close did Devon say anything, "What am I supposed to do?"

"Take orders, I'll make them today." Kieran unlocked the cafe and walked in. He went right to the sink and washed his hands before preparing the machines for the day.

Devon shook his head. "That's not what I mean. I'm a waste of space. I'm not even good here, I only make things worse for mom, and I'm not even a good omega."

Kieran looked at him directly. "It was one breakup. That doesn't mean your life is over."

"You have no idea how good he smelled. What if he was supposed to be my mate?" Devon sighed loudly and leaned against the counter.

"What if he just had nice cologne?" Kieran walked up and rested a hand on Devon's shoulder. "If it was meant to be, it'll find a way to work out. But also, don't be desperate for him. It was one guy, there are other alphas out there."

Devon nodded slowly. "Yeah, but where are the good ones?"

"I wish I knew." Kieran chuckled and went to the back room.

Devon took his place behind the register. They were open, but no one was coming in that early, so he could relax. His phone vibrated in his pocket. He pulled it out to see a text from Connor. He immediately locked the screen and angrily shoved it back in his pocket. Why was he texting him anyways? Did he want Devon for sex because Robbie wasn't going to put out? Devon smacked himself internally.

Luckily, as the day went on, more customers kept coming in and it turned out to be a pretty busy day. Devon didn't even think about Connor again. Several times throughout the day, he felt his phone vibrate repeatedly. But he chose to ignore it. Hopefully, it wasn't his mom. That would be bad. But he was almost certain it was Connor asking for something. It was pretty frustrating how Connor still had Devon's keys. Devon really didn't want to talk to him again, but his mom seemed to be pushing him to at least have a talk with Connor since she was making so many excuses about not getting him a new key.

He groaned. The lull between customers was leaving him time to think about that redhead again. On the bright side, Robbie wasn't working today so Devon had at least a moment of peace. Then his phone started vibrating again. Only this time, it wasn't just once and gone, it kept going. It was so annoying against his leg that he pulled his phone out of his pants pocket. Connor was calling him. "That desperate that you gave up on texting?" he mumbled to himself.

"Hmm?" Kieran looked up from the last drink he was making.

Devon shook his head. "Nothing. Can I take this call?"

Kieran nodded. "In the back."

Devon stepped into the back room. He took a breath before finally answering his phone. "Connor."

Connor's smooth voice reached Devon's ear, "Devon, I–"

He'd barely gotten two words out before Devon interrupted him. "I'm not your fuck toy."

There was a pause on the other end of the line. "What?"

"I know you're calling because Robbie wouldn't put out and you want someone to get you off, but I'm not your fuck toy. I'm worth more than that and I don't want to be used to being used for sex. I want more than that," Devon went on a long rant.

Connor sighed. Devon could imagine the look of disappointment that must be on the alpha's face. Connor finally said, "You don't know why I'm calling."

Devon furrowed his brow and grit his teeth. "I just said–"

"You just assumed," Connor corrected. "I ended that date with Robbie because I didn't want to be there."

"Maybe you're just saying that because you think it's what I want to hear."

"Devon, I'm not *your* fuck toy," Connor said without hesitation.

Devon stood up straighter. "What do you mean?"

"You were the one who asked for sex and you were the one who said we shouldn't be serious." Connor's voice was laced with sadness.

Devon took a step back and leaned against the wall. "I just thought... that's all alphas wanted, and..."

"I would've waited if you hadn't asked for it."

"Well, we'll never know now, will we?" Devon let out an audible breath and closed his eyes. Had he made things worse by keeping it casual? "But that doesn't explain why you were dating Robbie and me."

"I wasn't dating Robbie before yesterday. I didn't want you to run out."

"You called him sweetie." Devon gripped his phone tighter.

"I forgot his name," Connor responded immediately.

"Convenient…" Devon said quietly, but something told him that Connor was being honest.

"True." Connor let out another breath. "I didn't want to date Robbie. I wanted to make you jealous and as soon as you ran out of the cafe, I knew it was a mistake."

"I can't just be with you immediately after that…" Devon slumped down, crouching on the floor. He rubbed his temple.

"And I can't be in a casual relationship."

"Connor, I…" he trailed off, holding his phone away from his ear and hiding his face in his forearms. He wanted those strong arms and that smell of strawberry milk tea again. Kieran was wrong, there's no way that could've been cologne. It was his favorite smell and he wasn't imagining it. Your true mate was supposed to have a smell that you absolutely couldn't resist. Devon never thought it would be strawberry milk tea.

"Let me make it up to you." Connor speaking on the other side made Devon bring the phone back to his ear. "I'll take you out on a date tonight. I'll do whatever you want to do. I promise to take it slow if you promise to take us seriously."

Devon swallowed, why did he feel so choked up? He rubbed his eyes with the back of his hand. "I'll take it seriously, but I don't want to take it slow."

"Can I come see you today?"

Devon nodded even though Connor couldn't see it. "Come by the cafe at closing."

"I'll be there. Promise."

CHAPTER 18

"I'll see you tonight." Connor smiled, relaxing in his desk chair as he talked to Devon. Hearing his voice gave him hope again. Maybe things really could be different this time. Through the glass wall of his office, he saw Matt storming towards his office. Sammy stood up, trying to block him, but Matt snapped something and Sammy shrunk away.

Matt threw the door open and walked inside. "I've kept my mouth shut, but I can no longer be a party to this."

"The hell was that?" Devon's voice drifted into his ear again since Connor hadn't hung up yet. It was a good thing he was talking to Devon or he might've bitten Matt's head off. But the sweet sound of his smooth voice gave him one last grasp at calmness.

"There's a work issue. I'll be there tonight."

"Work issue? Yeah, I guess. I don't know how late I'll be here…" Devon's voice cracked and trailed off.

"Wait for me." Connor tried to sound as reassuring as he could, he did not need Matt ruining this second chance. He only heard silence in response. He pulled the phone away from his ear to see that Devon had already hung up. He gritted his jaw and very carefully set his phone on his desk. It was taking all of his self control to remain remotely calm.

"Kameron is tanking the engineering department." Matt snapped as soon as Connor put his phone down.

Connor fixed the three pens in his pen cup into a perfect triangle shape. Without looking up, he spoke, "Why, yes, Matt, please come into my office while I'm on an important phone call." He turned his gaze up to Matt, boring holes right into him.

Matt gulped, but took a step towards his desk. "This can't wait any longer. I haven't wanted to say anything against Kameron, but things are getting worse by the day and Kameron giving this new project to Tyler—."

"What's wrong with Tyler having work to do?" Connor cut Matt off mid sentence.

"Having work? He's getting all of the new projects while taking my team away from me?" Matt balled his hands into fists.

Connor looked at him with a rather bland expression. "How does this relate to Kameron?" He decided to humor Matt, wanting to see how far down this hole he'd dig himself. He seemed to want to rant rather than discuss anyways.

"He's making the same poor decisions for the tech stack. Forcing us to learn these new, untested languages is making our work more difficult than it needs to be. He's changed all of the projects and now I'm the only one on this project." Matt gestured aggressively.

"I'm sure it's because he thought you could handle a project on your own." Connor gave a taught smile, which the rest of his face did not match such an expression. He was doing his best to not engage in this fight that Matt clearly wanted to have. Despite the clear disrespect, Connor would not be baited with Matt's cheap words.

"Well... of course I *can*, but that's not the point!"

"Then what is?" Connor leaned back in his chair and crossed his arms.

"That Tyler is hardly qualified to manage people and Kameron gives him my whole team?" Matt's voice started to go up as he got angrier.

"Is Tyler unqualified?" Connor narrowed his eyes.

"Unqualified? He misses two to three days a month because of *omega problems*." Matt sneered.

Connor finally stood up, his shoulders back, towering over Matt as he glared down at him.

"I do not condone discrimination in this company."

"I'm just stating facts!"

Connor glared back at him, arms folded over his chest. "I expect you to treat Tyler the same as you would treat any of your other coworkers."

"So he gets my team just because he's an omega? Doesn't that seem like discrimination?"

"I'm sure he has his own team because of his own merits and you don't have yours because of your own actions." Connor would not be intimidated.

"If that's how you want to run your company, then I want no part of it." Matt stood up straighter. "I quit."

"Then consider this your last working day. Collect your things at the end of the day and leave your work laptop here." Honestly, Connor was relieved by this outcome. It saved him having to find a way to deal with such an unruly employee.

"Fine." Matt spun on his heel. He threw the door open again and stalked out.

Sammy poked his head in once Matt had gone. "Is everything alright, sir? I'm sorry I…"

"What did he say to you?" Connor walked over to Sammy, his brow knitted together.

"Just… I shouldn't get in his way…" Sammy looked to the side, wringing his hands.

"You're paraphrasing." Connor wanted a straight answer.

"An omega like me is supposed to listen to orders from an alpha like him…" Sammy still refused to look at Connor. "I shouldn't have stood back, but…"

"I don't blame you, Sammy." Connor let out a breath. "Can you get Kameron for me?"

Sammy nodded and quickly ducked out. Connor sat back down and leaned back in his chair. He ran a hand through his hair, taking a deep breath in and holding it for a moment before slowly letting his breath out. Matt was leaving, he didn't need to let the shit he pulled continue to annoy him. It still took Connor a minute to regain his composure before he could pull up a chart on his computer. He started to look over some of the company expenditures. Moments later, Kameron knocked on the office door as he opened it. "You asked for me?"

Connor looked up. He beckoned Kameron inside. "I have some news for you."

Kameron raised his brow. He walked in, carefully closing the door behind him and sat across from Connor. "Does it have to do with Matt? I'd be lying if I said I didn't notice the way he stormed in and then back out of here."

"He has put in his resignation." Connor shrugged. "Today's his last day."

Kameron blinked a few times. He leaned forward. "Really? So sudden? He didn't even tell me."

"I suspect that he thinks you should be the one leaving instead of him." Connor looked over the budget chart. "I know with the change in projects this last week or so, the engineering team has been working a lot better."

Kameron nodded. "We actually get a lot more done when Matt is on his own and not micromanaging his team."

"Taking into account his project, do you think it's something your team can handle?"

"I don't see why not." Kameron shrugged.

Connor smiled. "Good, then I won't be hiring a replacement for Matt yet. I think we should see how the team goes." And saving the company one less engineer salary would help them meet their quarterly earnings a little easier.

"I'll go talk to the team." Kameron stood up. "That is if Matt hasn't made his own announcement already."

"Good luck." Connor chuckled.

• • •

Connor's feet pounded the pavement as he jogged the few blocks between his office building and Almond Blossom Tea. After their phone call earlier, Connor didn't bother to wait until closing, but rather came directly here after he'd finished up his work for the day. His heart was beating fast and his breathing was hard. It wasn't that he was out of shape, but rather, what if Devon had already gone home for the day? Connor couldn't bear the thought. He stopped one shopfront down from the cafe and took a deep breath. He kept holding his breath as he walked into the cafe, hoping that Devon would be there to greet him.

He walked inside the cafe and his heart plummeted. He saw a man about his age at the register. The man looked familiar, but he didn't know his name. Connor glanced behind him, but didn't see Robbie or Devon. Still, he walked up to the register. The man smiled and asked, "How can I help you?"

"Is Devon here?" His brow furrowed. There was a clear sense of urgency in his voice.

"You must be Connor!" The man smiled. He nodded. "He's in the back. I'll go tell him you're here."

He let out a breath of relief. If this guy was relaxed and smiling, then that had to be a good sign, right? "I don't mind waiting until his shift is done. I can get a drink." He smiled, pulling out his wallet.

"Well, if you want something to drink, I won't stop you, but he's ready to go whenever."

Connor nodded. Despite smelling that this man was an omega, Connor could sense an air of authority about him. "In that case, I'll take two strawberry milk teas and one Devon."

The man chuckled as he rang up the order. "I'll have those right out for you."

Connor nodded and stepped to the side after paying. The man went into the back room, so he impatiently waited at the pick-up counter, constantly staring at the door as if he could manifest Devon to walk through it. After what seemed like an eternity, Devon did indeed emerge through the doorway. Connor grinned wider. Devon walked up to him at the pick-up counter. "A part of me wondered if you would still show up."

"And miss seeing the cutest omega ever?" He held his hands out, offering them to Devon.

At first, Devon looked at the hands, but then he slowly placed his hands in Connor's. "Do you just want me for my looks?"

"I want to get to know all of you," Connor smiled, "especially now that we're dating."

"Dating…" A faint blush creeped over Devon's cheeks.

"You did say that you didn't want to take things slow." Connor leaned forward, hoping that Devon still felt that way.

Devon nodded slowly, glancing up at Connor. "It's just new to me. I haven't dated before."

"Then be prepared to be swept off your feet." Connor rubbed the back of Devon's hands with his thumbs.

"Promise?" Devon glanced up at Connor.

"Promise." Connor smiled.

"Two strawberry milk teas." The omega walking up with their drinks made Devon blush more and take a step back from Connor, snatching his hands away.

"Sorry, I'll get back to work." Devon looked away from both of them.

The other man shook his head. "You're free to head out."

"Really?" Devon's head snapped up.

"Yes." He chuckled. "You should go before I change my mind."

Devon grinned. "Thanks." He ducked into the backroom once more, returning with his jacket. He skipped out from behind the counter and to Connor's side.

Connor held out one of the drinks Devon. He looked him up and down. "Weren't you wearing that yesterday?"

Devon took the drink with both hands and looked away as he headed for the door. "Yeah, well… after I ran out last night, my boss found me and let me crash at his place."

Connor rested his free hand on Devon's back. "Don't run out on me again, okay?"

"Don't go on a date with someone else again. You said you wanted this to be serious, so it's just you and me now, okay?" Devon took a long sip of the pink drink.

"I wouldn't have it any other way." Connor smiled.

"So um…" Devon looked up to Connor. "What're we doing anyways?"

"I thought you might be hungry, can I take you out to eat?"

"I wouldn't mind eating what you make. I… wish I'd stayed for breakfast." Devon looked away again, but Connor saw the faint dusting of pink on his cheeks. He couldn't resist and leaned over to gently kiss that red cheek. Devon started a bit, the blush intensifying as he touched a hand to his own cheek.

Connor wrapped his arm around Devon's back and started walking in the direction of his apartment building. "Then I wouldn't mind cooking breakfast for you, too."

"I-I'm not a slut or something, I just…" Devon covered his face with his palm.

Connor chuckled. "I want you, too, and only you. Don't worry about anything for now."

CHAPTER 19

Devon once again stepped into Connor's posh apartment. He wasn't making quite the fool of himself this time. At least, he hoped not. He walked in and sat on the couch. He hadn't actually spent a lot of time in this room before. It was definitely a comfortable living space despite being so tidy. The navy blue couches faced the large windows, it was nice to sit here and enjoy such a view of Mount Oolie. Maybe Devon was more relaxed this time and could actually appreciate being here.

Connor walked around to join him by the couch and smiled down at him. "What would you like? I can make a few things."

Devon bit his lip and reached up to gently grab Connor's shirt and pulled him closer. "I'm not really hungry right now, but I want breakfast."

Connor gulped, his Adam's apple bobbing up and down. He knelt down in front of Devon. "Promise you'll stay."

Devon nodded, smiling a little as he glanced into Connor's eyes and quickly glanced away. "Promise."

Connor leaned forward, cupping Devon's cheek in his hand and pressing his lips against his. Devon closed his eyes and rested his hand over Connor's. Those warm lips tasted just like strawberry milk tea. He moved his hands to hold Connor's face, feeling the stubble along his jaw. He was so perfectly handsome.

Connor rubbed his free hand over Devon's thigh, slowly making his way higher each time. Devon gasped into the kiss when he felt Connor's hand brush between his legs. His first reaction was to bring his knees together, but Connor had already seated himself right between his legs. Devon could only clench onto Connor's sides with his knees. Connor didn't seem phased at all. He kept placing tender kisses on Devon's lips. His hand rubbed Devon between his legs, making Devon let out more soft moans. He desperately wanted to get his pants out of the way, but Connor seemed happy to take his time.

"Co—" Devon pulled back from the kiss with a gasp.

Connor didn't stop, he moved to kiss Devon's cheek and down to his neck, leaving Devon's skin tingling under each kiss. Devon tilted his head to give Connor better access to his neck. He knotted his fingers in the alpha's hair. He bit his lip, trying to keep his voice in, feeling embarrassed about the sounds he heard himself making. But that didn't keep him from pushing his hips up against Connor's hand.

Connor let out a short chuckle. "Getting impatient?"

"No…" Devon lied, looking away, his face a bright red.

Connor kissed his way up to Devon's ear and whispered, "Will you trust me?"

Devon nodded.

Without another word, Connor slipped his hands under Devon's ass and lifted him up. Devon clung onto Connor with his arms and legs. Connor chuckled again as he walked them out of the living room. Devon kept his face buried in Connor's shoulder. Next thing he knew, Connor was laying him down on the bed. Devon kept blushing, turning his head and covering his face with his arms.

Connor wiggled Devon's pants off. "You're really cute when you're shy."

Devon brought his arms closer together. "D-don't say such cheesy things like that!"

"But you seem to like it." Connor pressed his large, warm hand against Devon's exposed abdomen. Devon bit his lip and closed his eyes, trying to remain in control of himself. A soft pair of lips on his skin made him gasp out loud. Connor's voice was low as he spoke, "You act like you're unshakable and unafraid. This feels like a whole new side of you."

"That counts as more cheesy things." It's not like Devon didn't love the sweet words, but he didn't know how to respond. Should he say thank you? Try and deny it? Luckily, he didn't have to think about it, Connor was already leaning up and peeling his arms away as he leaned in for another kiss. Devon readily kissed him back, holding his face close again.

Connor's hands explored all of Devon's skin, exposing more and more of him as he moved the clothes out of the way. As Devon continued to focus on the kiss, he was able to relax more and to let his hands slide down Connor's neck. Then he brought his hands forward onto Connor's chest and slowly undid each button of his shirt. With all of the buttons undone, he slipped his hands under the shirt and over Connor's shoulders, pushing the shirt off. He let his hands linger over Connor's strong arms. Even though this alpha ran a company, he took the time to take care of himself. Connor's arms were well-defined and strong. He loved the way he could feel the alpha's power when Connor grabbed his hips.

Indulging in this sweet moment, he did feel like he could truly trust Connor. Especially since Connor was treating him so tenderly. Every movement, every touch was filled with love. Devon didn't want to say that he was falling for the redhead, but he'd be lying if he said his heart didn't feel lighter around Connor.

Connor was careful to make sure that Devon was well prepared before connecting with him. Devon kept clinging onto him, unable to control his voice and letting out breathy moans against Connor's ear. Connor gripped onto Devon's hips tighter as they moved together. Devon's voice got louder. He couldn't keep in how good he was feeling. Connor knew every spot that made him weak and how to get him to lose control.

He dug his fingers into Connor's shoulders, arched his back, even his toes curled. "Connor, I can't... I—"

Connor held him closer and placed a bunch of little kisses all over Devon's neck.

Devon couldn't hold back. The pleasure was too overwhelming. His mind was filled with Connor and nothing else. His breath left his body and he couldn't get it back. All he could do was cling onto Connor like his life depended on it. And Connor cradled him back, keeping their bodies flush against each other the whole time.

● ● ●

Sunlight started to stream into the room and woke Devon. He rubbed his eyes. He felt that he was in the bed alone. He sat up and looked around, he'd taken all the covers and the spot next to him was cold. "Connor?"

He pulled the covers tighter around himself, feeling suddenly cold. He didn't want to get up and walk around naked. He glanced around the room, trying to find his clothes. Where did Connor go anyways?

"Connor?" He called out again, his voice more strained.

Moments later, Connor rushed into the room. His face was etched with worry as he went straight to Devon's side and sat next to him. "What's wrong?"

Devon blushed, staring at Connor for a moment. He bit his lip and looked away as he shook his head. "N-nothing... I just... you weren't here and so I—"

"Devon," Connor cut him off and rested his hand on Devon's cheek, "I'm not going anywhere." He leaned his forehead against Devon's.

"You better not." Devon nuzzled his forehead against Connor's. He really couldn't explain the surprisingly light and happy feeling in his heart.

"Breakfast is almost ready, want to eat in bed?" Connor caressed Devon's cheek.

Devon shook his head. "Let's go out to the kitchen." He couldn't deny that he was hungry. He ended up falling asleep pretty soon after they'd finished last night. Connor stood up and offered his hand to help Devon up. Devon chuckled. "If you spoil me too much, I might start getting used to it."

"Then get used to it." Connor smiled and helped Devon out of bed.

Devon quickly picked up the first article of clothing he could find. It just happened to be Connor's shirt that was laying at the foot of the bed. He pulled it over his head, taking a sniff of the shirt. Strawberry milk tea. He glanced up to see Connor staring at him, eyes wide. Devon scratched the back of his neck. "Sorry, I can find something else."

Connor shook his head. He stepped in and pulled Devon closer by his waist. "I didn't expect you to do something like that. You're tempting me to skip breakfast." Connor leaned in, kissing Devon's neck and taking a long sniff.

Devon bit his lip, resting his hands on Connor's shoulders. "You're making it hard to resist, yourself." But Devon's stomach audibly growled. His face instantly turned pink and he hid his face against Connor's shoulder.

Connor laughed. "It seems that food definitely needs to be first." He kept his arm wrapped around Devon's waist as he escorted him to the kitchen. He only let go when they were inside. He went directly to the stove and picked up two plates. "I made a lot, so eat as much as you want."

Devon smiled and sat at the table. He took a long sniff. It smelled just as good as before. It made him even hungrier. "I might just take you up on that." He started to eat, taking a big first bite. "Mm! This is delicious!" He glanced over at Connor, who was staring at him, not even touching his plate. Devon furrowed his brow. "Is yours cold or something?"

Connor looked down at his plate and back at Devon. "I like to see you happily eating my food."

Devon looked away, food still in his mouth as he mumbled, "It's your fault for making something so tasty."

Connor reached across the table and took hold of Devon's hand. He quickly swallowed and looked down at their hands. Connor caressed the back of Devon's hand with his thumb. "I'm glad you stayed."

Devon held his hand back tightly. "I'm glad you still wanted me to."

"I'll always want you to stay." Connor's voice was completely serious, not a hint of joking in it.

"Always is a long time." Devon kept looking at their hands, avoiding eye contact. It would be too easy to give in to forever if he looked back at the alpha.

But Connor wasn't put off in the least. "I want a long time."

"What if I get boring or too weird or—"

"What if I get more interested in you every time I see you?" Connor interrupted him.

Devon finally looked up at the alpha. Their eyes met and he could feel the intensity of Connor's gaze right to his core. Deep down, he knew Connor was serious and he'd be lying if he said that he didn't feel the same. "I want a long time, too."

Connor smiled and leaned across the table. Their lips met in a soft, sweet kiss.